Gargoyles
of
Gaylord

**Look for more 'American Chillers®'
from AudioCraft Publishing, Inc.,
coming soon! And don't forget to pick up
these books in Johnathan Rand's thrilling
'Michigan Chillers' series:**

#1: Mayhem on Mackinac Island
#2: Terror Stalks Traverse City
#3: Poltergeists of Petoskey
#4: Aliens Attack Alpena
#5: Gargoyles of Gaylord
#6: Strange Spirits of St. Ignace
#7: Kreepy Klowns of Kalamazoo
#8: Dinosaurs Destroy Detroit
#9: Sinister Spiders of Saginaw
#10: Mackinaw City Mummies

American Chillers:
#1: The Michigan Mega-Monsters
#2: Ogres of Ohio
#3: Florida Fog Phantoms
#4: New York Ninjas
#5: Terrible Tractors of Texas
#6: Invisible Iguanas of Illinois
#7: Wisconsin Werewolves
#8: Minnesota Mall Mannequins
#9: Iron Insects Invade Indiana
#10: Missouri Madhouse
#11: Poisonous Pythons Paralyze Pennsylvania
#12: Dangerous Dolls of Delaware

and more coming soon!

AudioCraft Publishing, Inc.
PO Box 281
Topinabee Island, MI 49791

#5: Gargoyles
of
Gaylord

JOHNATHAN RAND

An AudioCraft Publishing, Inc. book

Graphics layout/design consultant: Chuck Beard, Straits Area Printing

ISBN 1-893699-10-2

Printed in USA

Fourth Printing January 2004

Gargoyles of Gaylord

Visit the official 'American Chillers' web site at:

www.americanchillers.com

Featuring excerpts from upcoming stories, interviews, contests, official American Chillers wearables, and *more!* Plus, join the FREE American Chillers fan club!

1

The first thing you need to know about me is that I am afraid of the dark. Dark rooms, dark hallways, dark stairs . . . I'm just afraid of the dark, period.

I think a lot of people are afraid of the dark, but they just don't admit it.

But I have a reason to be afraid! You would have a reason, too, if you knew what I went through last summer.

My name is Corrine. Corrine MacArthur.

But everybody calls me Corky. In fact, not many people even know my real name. Everybody — even my school teachers — call me Corky. Actually, I kind of like the nickname.

Corky.

I haven't always been afraid of the dark. Up until last summer, I don't think I was afraid of the dark at all.

But something happened last summer that changed all that.

It was the middle of June, and school had just gotten out. It was the beginning of summer. I love summer! The days are longer and warmer, and there's so much to do. We live in Gaylord, which is a small city in the middle of northern lower Michigan. Gaylord is called 'The Alpine Village'. A lot of buildings in town are built to look like the buildings in Switzerland, and every summer there's a big festival called 'Alpenfest'. Thousands of people come from all over to celebrate. It's pretty cool.

In the summertime, I get to stay out late. Well, later than we get to stay out during the school year. All of my friends on the block get together and play yard games like 'kick the can' and 'ghost in the graveyard.' We play till long after dark.

On this particular night, there was about ten of us playing outside. It had just gotten dark, and the streetlight was on. We had just finished playing a game, and my friend Ashley and I were sitting on the curb, watching giant June bugs swarm around the street light. June bugs are noisy . . . they sound like little airplanes flying through the sky. Their wings clap like playing cards clipped between bicycle spokes.

"Well, I'd better get home," Ashley said. "I'm supposed to be home by ten."

"See ya later," I said, standing up. A lock of my black hair fell in front of my face, and I brushed it away. I started walking across our yard, then I stopped and turned back around. "You want to go to the park with us tomorrow?" I asked Ashley. We don't live too far from the park. There's a creek there, and a big field. I like to wade in the creek and catch crayfish. Ashley thinks they're gross. But we always have a lot of fun.

She stopped and turned.

"Yeah, sure," she replied. "See you at the park in the morning." And with that, she turned and began walking home. She lives only a few houses down from us.

The night was unusually dark. There was no

moon, and the day had been cloudy. The sky above had no stars. But the street light lit up everything in the yard.

I was almost to our porch when all of a sudden, everything went black!

The lights . . . all of them . . . went out! The street lights, the porch light, all of the lights in our house . . . even the lights in the other houses on the street . . . went out!

I was in total darkness!

Now remember . . . at this time, I wasn't afraid of the dark. It sure was strange that all of the lights went off like that. But it's happened before. In Gaylord, we can get some pretty fierce snowstorms in the winter. Once in a while, the power will go out. It's kind of fun, really. Dad will light a fire in the fireplace, and sometimes we even cook hot dogs and marshmallows. It makes me wish we had snowstorms more often.

But this was the middle of summer. It was

strange that the power just went off like that.

And it was *dark!* It was darker than I had ever seen before. I couldn't see the porch ten feet in front of me. I couldn't see any trees. I couldn't see anything.

I stopped dead in my tracks. I didn't want to accidentally smack into the porch or into a tree.

I turned, looking down the street . . . or, where I *thought* the street should be. It was far too dark to see the street or any street signs.

I wondered what caused all of the lights to go off. Maybe there was a problem at the power plant. Maybe the whole city was out of power!

All of a sudden, I heard Ashley's voice calling out.

"Corky?!?!" she shouted. "Are you still outside?!?!?" Her voice echoed down the street.

"Yes!" I shouted back.

"It sure is dark!" she hollered.

"Like 'duh'!" I replied loudly. "It's a power failure. I don't see any lights on anywhere."

"I can't even see my own house!" she shouted.

"Me neither!" I shouted back. "And I'm only ten feet away from it!"

"Too bad it isn't Halloween," she laughed.

Ashley has this really funny giggle, and it sounded even funnier, echoing down the street. It was like there were two or three Ashley's laughing. It sure was strange, standing here in the dark and talking to her without being able to see her.

"Well, I'm going to try and make it to my house," she said. "But it's so dark, I can't even see my nose!"

"Be careful of Mr. Hansel's house," I said loudly. "I hear that he eats kids!"

"Knock it off!" she shouted back to me. "That's just a story!"

Mr. Hansel is a strange man that lives in the house next to Ashley's. We hardly ever see him, and he only leaves his house at night. Someone made up a story that he eats children, but I've never believed it.

What's even weirder is that Mr. Hansel has a fenced in back yard. But it's not just a fence . . . it's a wooden fence. It's almost eight feet tall, and you can't even see through it. There's no telling what he has in his back yard. Some people say that there's an old graveyard back there. Other people say that they hear strange noises coming from behind the fence, but they don't know what they are. One of my friends at school swears that he saw Mr. Hansel actually climb over the fence! That would be almost impossible! I mean . . . Mr. Hansel is old . . . and the fence is taller than he is!

There are other stories, too. Some people say that Mr. Hansel is a troll that can turn into any kind of animal that he wants.

But those are just stories. Nobody can do stuff like that. When I was little, I used to believe the stories. I thought that they were real.

I've only seen Mr. Hansel a few times. He's got messy gray hair, and he stoops forward when he walks. And he's always got a mean look on his face.

At least, whenever I've seen him, he's got a mean look on his face! Mr. Hansel doesn't look like a nice man. In fact, he looks scary. Scary and mean.

"I'll see you later," Ashley shouted one final time from a few houses down.

"Later," I shouted back, and I began walking carefully through the darkness to the porch.

In the next instant, a shrill scream pierced the dark night! It was a long, painful wail that echoed up and down the street!

Ashley!

Ashley's scream rang down the block, echoing like the Grand Canyon.

"Ashley!" I screamed. *"What's wrong?!?"*

But she didn't answer me. She just screamed and screamed and screamed.

Suddenly, her screaming stopped. Her voice was cut short, like someone . . . or something . . . had stopped her.

What could I do? It was too dark to see anything.

But I had to help Ashley. Something had happened, and I was sure that she needed help.

"Ashley?" I called out, taking a few brave steps in her direction. I strained my eyes to see her, but it was no use. It was just too dark.

"Ashley?" I called out again.

No answer. What had happened to her?

I began walking faster, hoping that I wouldn't trip or smack into something in the dark.

I walked across our driveway, and then felt my sneakers sink back into the squishy grass. I took a few steps, then stopped.

I could hear moaning coming from the next yard. It was muffled and soft, and it was hard to hear, but I knew who it was.

Ashley.

She was hurt!

Without thinking, I took off running blindly through the dark.

"Ashley!" I shouted. "Where are you?!? Where are you?!?!"

More moaning.

I took off running again, but I didn't get far. I had only taken about four steps when my foot caught on something and I stumbled, falling forward. I raised my hands out in front of me as I fell, and I hit the ground with a heavy thud.

"Oooof!" I said, as the wind was knocked out of me.

"Ouch!" Ashley groaned.

I had tripped over her!

"Are you okay?" I said, getting to my knees.

"Yeah, I think so," she said. Her voice was tight and I could tell she was hurting. "But it didn't help when you ran into me."

"Well, how was I supposed to know that you were on the grass?" I snapped. "It's so dark, I can't see a thing."

All of a sudden a loud 'pop!' filled the air, and all of the lights came back on! The streetlight in front of our house shined brightly in the night, and windows from houses glowed a creamy yellow.

And for the first time, I realized we were in Mr. Hansel's yard.

I stood up and walked over to Ashley.

There was blood on her leg! Just above her knee, she had a nasty scrape.

"Yuuuuck," I said. "Does it hurt bad?"

"It did for a minute," she answered. "For a minute, it really hurt bad."

"Hold on a second," I said, peering at the wound on her leg. "Look. It almost looks like you've been bitten by something."

Ashley kneeled forward, looking at the scrape on her leg. There appeared to be two deep gashes — bite marks — that had punctured the skin.

"That's gross," she said. "It's gross and it hurts."

"What did you scrape it on?" I asked, turning.

"That," Ashley pointed. "Right there."

I turned and looked at the shadowy form she was pointing to. I hadn't seen it earlier. Actually, I didn't remember ever seeing it there before. In fact, I was *certain* that I hadn't seen it before.

I walked closer to the object. It was about half my height, and about as big around as a beach ball.

What in the world, I thought.

But when I got closer, I knew what it was.

A gargoyle.

I drew a sudden, quick breath, and covered my mouth with my hand.

A gargoyle.

Not a real gargoyle, of course . . . but one of those stone ones that you see in gardens. They're just statues, but some of them sure look real.

And this one looked *very* real, that's for sure.

It was all gray, made out of cement. It had a fat face with a pudgy nose. Sharp, piercing eyes glared back at me. In its mouth were four angry fangs . . . two on the top and two on the bottom. Two thick wings grew from its back. The gargoyle was in a hunched position, as if it was about to fly.

"What is it?" Ashley asked, finally getting to her feet. She held one hand near her wound as she limped toward me.

"A cement gargoyle," I replied, still staring at the statue. I knew it wasn't real, but it just looked so weird. It looked so real, even though it was only made out of cement. I kept staring at it. I had never seen it in the yard before.

"Eeeeww, that's gross," Ashley said as she stopped at my side. "What would Mr. Hansel be doing with a gargoyle in his yard?"

"Who knows?" I replied. "Nothing that Mr. Hansel does makes any sense, anyway."

I couldn't stop staring at the statue. Something in its mouth caught my attention. Suddenly, I knew what it was.

"Ashley . . . look at that," I said quietly. "Look in its mouth."

Ashley leaned closer. "What?" she asked.

"Look in its mouth," I repeated. "Look at its teeth!"

She bent closer.

"That's even MORE gross!" she said loudly,

shivering.

On one of the teeth, a tiny blood stain remained.

Ashley's blood.

"That must be where I ran into him," Ashley said, glancing down at the wound on her leg.

"Yeah," I replied. "Either that . . . or he BIT YOU!" As I said the words *'bit you'*, I suddenly grabbed Ashley with both hands around her waist. She shrieked and doubled over. We both laughed and laughed.

"I gotta go," she finally said. She bent her head down, inspecting the wound on her leg. "I've got to get this cleaned before it gets infected."

"And before you get bit again," I laughed. Ashley laughed, too. "See you tomorrow," I said, and I watched her as she walked across the darkened yard toward her house. When I saw her shadow reach her porch, I hollered out.

"Bye!" I shouted.

"See you tomorrow!" she said. I heard the front door of her house open, and light streamed out. The door closed with a thud.

The night was quiet. Singing crickets filled the air, and the sound of cars traveling on nearby Otsego street were the only things I could hear.

And so, as I stood in the dim light of the street lamp, the sound of fluttering wings close by caused me to nearly jump out of my skin.

I spun, and what I saw almost made me faint.

The cement gargoyle that had been sitting in the yard had taken flight!

It was enormous! Its wings beat the air like a giant owl, and it spun through the sky with the speed of a bat!

I couldn't believe what I was seeing. The gargoyle swung out of sight in the shadows, then suddenly came back into view as it dipped beneath the street light in front of our house. Then it wheeled back around, its wings outstretched, swooping through the sky. I could only see its shadow, but I didn't need to see any more. It was flying faster, zipping through the night sky like a mad hornet. I could hear its wings pounding the air like a drum.

Wha-whoosh . . . wha-whoosh . . . .

Closer . . . .

Wha-whoosh . . . wha-whoosh . . . .

Closer . . . .

Wha-whoosh . . . wha-whoosh . . . .

Closer still!

Oh no! It was coming for me!

5

The gargoyle was only a few feet from me when I dove to the grass, face first. I held out my arms in front of me to break my fall, then I rolled sideways. I could hear the huge beast swoop over me and pass by.

Whew! That had been close.

But there was still danger! The gargoyle was still in the sky . . . and he was coming after me!

I couldn't see the creature, but I could still hear the thundering of wings as the gargoyle spun in the air above me. I started rolling on the grass, hoping that if I kept moving, the awful creature wouldn't be able to get me. The grass was dew-covered and it soaked my skin and my clothes. I kept rolling, frantically twisting and turning, rolling to who knows where. I just wanted to keep moving—away from the gargoyle!

This was crazy! There is no such thing as gargoyles! Not *real* ones, anyway. Gargoyles are just make-believe, like fairy tails and cartoons and elves. They aren't supposed to be real!

Are they?

I kept rolling, but I could still hear the thunder of wings above me. I knew that the gargoyle was only a few feet overhead.

I hit something, and it stopped my roll.

A tree! I had rolled into a tree!

I leapt to my feet, clenching my fists, anxiously scanning the sky, searching for the gargoyle.

This was impossible. Worse! It was unbelievable! A stone gargoyle had come to life—and was flying around! I thought this stuff only happened in the movies!

It certainly wasn't supposed to happen in Gaylord!

I saw the gargoyle fly by again, and I ducked behind the tree. I could hear a loud flapping of wings as the beast circled the tree, over and over again, around and around and around.

Then, as quickly as it had attacked, I heard it flying away. I saw its shadow as it flew toward the street light, then it flew off and up into the night. Soon, the only sounds I heard were crickets and the gentle hum of cars from downtown.

Was the gargoyle gone? If he was, where did he go?

I backed out from beneath the tree, my head upturned, searching the dark sky for the gargoyle. Thankfully, I didn't see it.

I walked over to the spot where the gargoyle had been perched on the lawn. The grass was matted and all crushed down like you would expect. It looked like two big feet had pressed down into the grass.

Again, I looked up, my eyes searching the night sky.

No gargoyle.

Had this really happened? How did a cement gargoyle come to life and fly away? Was it really cement, after all?

I looked back at Mr. Hansel's house. It was

all dark except for one small window that glowed from a light inside. I hope he hadn't heard me. If Mr. Hansel caught me in his yard, I would be a dead duck!

I guess I'd better go home, I thought. *I can figure this out in the morning, when there's more light.*

I was about to turn and walk home when, out of nowhere, two claws suddenly grasped my shoulders from behind!

I jumped out of my skin, spinning around, ready to run as fast as I could.

"Hey, you. I was wondering where you went. Sorry to scare you."

It was Dad! Claws hadn't grabbed me, after all. They were just Dad's hands. Boy, was I glad it was him!

"You didn't scare me," I stammered. Dad grinned, and I smiled, too. "Well, not very much, anyway," I finished.

"Your mother has been looking for you. She said something about a TV program that you wanted to watch."

"Oh, yeah," I said. "Thanks." Actually, I couldn't remember what show it was that I wanted to watch. I think it was some scary movie or something.

But I think I'd had enough scary things happen to me for one night!

"Dad . . . did you see anything out here just now? You know . . . like . . . in the sky?"

He looked at me and frowned. "Like what?" he asked.

"Oh, I don't know. Like a . . . a big owl," I finished.

"No, I didn't see anything. Why? Did you see one?"

"Oh, no . . . I mean . . . I think so . . . but I'm not sure."

"Well, there are a lot of owls around. We usually don't see many here in the city, but it's possible."

But I knew that what I had seen wasn't an owl.

It was a gargoyle. I *knew* it was.

■ ● ● ● ● ●|

The next morning I got up early. Actually, I always get up early. I'm always up before Mom or Dad, and even my little brother, Steven. He usually gets up early to watch cartoons.

Mornings are my favorite time of the day. Most of my friends tell me that they like to sleep in, but I don't. I like to get up early. It's the only part of the day that's so quiet and fresh and new. Nobody bugs me about anything. How could they? They're still sleeping.

And this morning, I had completely forgotten all about last night.

Until I went outside.

The birds were singing, but the sun wasn't quite up yet. The air was crisp and clean, and a bit cool. I was glad I had put on a heavy sweatshirt.

I jumped off the porch, found my bike in the garage, and hopped on it. A bike ride around the block and down by the park would be fun, even this early in the morning.

But when I pulled out of my driveway and began peddling along the sidewalk, my eyes caught something in a yard up ahead.

In Mr. Hansel's yard.

Gargoyles.

Not just one . . . but *two!*

I hit the brakes and stopped, staring at the two large, cement lawn statues perched in the center of the wet lawn.

The memories of last night came flooding back to me: Ashley's 'bite' mark, the gargoyle flying off into the night, swooping over me. And now there were *two* gargoyles hunched in Mr. Hansel's yard.

Had he placed another one there in the middle of the night? Even if he did, how did a cement yard statue come alive? Had I been dreaming?

No, I was sure I hadn't. I remembered the short power failure. I remembered Dad coming to find me. I remembered *everything* about last night. There's no way I had been dreaming.

I kept wondering, as I balanced myself on the motionless bicycle, how a cement gargoyle could come alive. It had to be some sort of trick. It had to be some sort of trick . . . but I had to find out for sure.

I hopped off my bike and held it by the handlebars, walking along the sidewalk until I was directly in front of Mr. Hansel's yard. Then I laid my bike down on the sidewalk and walked slowly toward the gargoyles. The grass was wet and my sneakers were soaked through after only a few steps.

I guess the gargoyles really *did* look real. I could see the ripples of what looked like wrinkled skin. But it wasn't skin, of course . . . it was cement.

And their eyes. They seemed to be looking at me, glaring at me as I came closer. The gargoyles really did look real.

But I knew they weren't. When I got close to them, it was easy to see that they were made out of cement. Cement animals don't come to life.

Maybe on TV they do, but not in real life.

And looking at their open mouths, it was easy to see how Ashley could have gotten hurt. Their teeth hung out of their mouths, and anyone walking along who hadn't seen the statue sitting there could have easily bumped up against it, scraping their leg. That's what Ashley had done. It was so dark last night that she hadn't seen the gargoyle, and she bumped into it with her leg. Plus, she was wearing shorts, so that didn't help. I had been wearing jeans last night. If I had bumped into the gargoyle, I don't think it would have even scraped my skin.

I turned away, giggled, and began walking back to my bike. The gargoyle that I had seen flying in the air last night had only been my imagination. It's funny how your mind can play tricks on you like that, and make things that aren't there seem real.

But how did the *second* gargoyle get there? That was a mystery . . . but I was sure there was some reasonable answer.

I was almost to my bike when I froze. I had heard something behind me.

Grrrrrrrrrrrrrroooowwwwww . . . .

It was a deep, growling snarl.

Grrrrrrrrrrrrrroooowwwwww . . . .

It was a deep, growling snarl . . . and it was real!

7

I spun, fearing the worst. I thought that maybe somehow, someway, the gargoyles might really be alive.

Maybe they weren't statues after all.

I looked at the two gargoyles. They were still sitting in the yard, in the same spot they had been a few moments before.

But now there was another figure in the yard.

Mr. Hansel! He was the one who had made that weird growling noise! He must have seen me!

Again, he made this weird snarling sound, like an animal. Mr. Hansel is freaky. His hair was all gray and messy like it always is, and he was wearing a long white coat. He looked like he was a mad scientist or something. And in the dim gray of early morning, he looked creepy.

"YOU!" he hissed. "WHAT ARE YOU DOING HERE?!?!"

"N . . . nothing," I stammered. "Umm, nothing, really."

"What are you doing in my yard?" he demanded. He started walking toward me.

"I, uh, umm—"

"*Answer me!*" he insisted again. He was mean. The closer he came, the meaner he looked. His eyes were big and beady, and his cheeks were red with anger.

I slowly took a step backwards, my eyes still glued to Mr. Hansel. I knew I wasn't far from my bicycle. I thought about running to my bike, hopping on it, and speeding off. There is no way Mr. Hansel could catch me. I can ride really fast on my bike.

But now there was no time. I had always thought Mr. Hansel was slow, but he was already across the yard. His bug eyes glared at me.

Suddenly, he was leering over me, pointing a bony finger in my face.

"Listen here you," he hissed silently. He squinted his eyes as he spoke, and his face was only inches away from mine. *"You stay out of this yard. You stay out of this yard forever. Do you understand?"*

I was too afraid to move, but I managed to nod my head. I understood, all right.

"That's goooood," he sneered, inching closer. *"Because we wouldn't want you to wind up like those two over there, now, would we?"* He pointed to the two gargoyles sitting in the yard.

Oh my gosh! Had he turned someone into gargoyles?!?! Had the gargoyles in the yard been people at one time?!?!

I couldn't stand it any longer. I had to get away.

Without another thought, I spun on my heels and bolted to my bike. I snatched it up off the ground, hopped on it, and began peddling as fast as I could.

"That's it," Mr Hansel yelled as I rode off. I could hear his voice echoing down the street. *"Ride! Ride as fast as you can!"* He laughed a terrible, wicked laugh. *"Because when they come for you, there will be no way to escape! And they're coming for you,*

Corky! The gargoyles . . . they're coming for yooouuu!
Very sooooon, Corky! Veeeryy soooonnn . . . ."

His shouting faded as I turned the corner around the block. I peddled like mad, not slowing down until I was sure I was a long ways away.

Finally, I stopped at the park. My heart thumped in my chest and my breathing was quick.

What did Mr. Hansel mean? Gargoyles were coming for me? *Real* gargoyles? There's no such thing. Did Mr. Hansel mean the gargoyles in his yard? That was crazy! I'm not afraid of cement lawn statues!

But I *was* afraid of Mr. Hansel. The way he looked at me like he did. He looked freaky! He scared me more than any gargoyle would. I wasn't afraid of a silly statue.

But that night, something awful happened that changed my mind!

Here's what happened:

Later in the morning, I went to Ashley's house. We rode our bikes all the way to Mossback Creek, which is about two miles from where we live. I told her about what had happened early that morning in Mr. Hansel's yard.

"You're kidding!" she said, her eyes wide. I shook my head.

"Nope," I said. "He was really freaky. All of those stories we've heard about him . . . maybe they're true after all."

"But what did he mean when he said that the gargoyles were coming to get you?" Ashley asked.

"I think he was just trying to scare us," I said. "I think he just wants us to stay out of his yard."

"He doesn't have to tell me twice," Ashley said, pointing to the scrape on her bare leg. Actually, she wasn't hurt that bad. There was just a red scrape mark on her skin where she had bumped into the cement gargoyle. It could have been a lot worse. She could have broken her leg if she'd hit the statue any harder.

"But there is something else I haven't told you," I said. When I explained to her what I saw last night — the flying gargoyle — she cringed.

"Are you sure?" she asked, eyes wide, her voice just above a whisper.

"Well, I guess I don't know. But I was sure at the time. It really scared me."

"Do you think it was real?" she replied.

I shrugged. "It sure looked real. It flew all around the yard and under the street light. It was huge! I could hear its wings beating the air and everything. It looked like it was a real gargoyle. But there's only one way to find out."

"How?" Ashley asked.

"Well, there's something going on at Mr. Hansel's. We don't know how that gargoyle got into his yard in the first place. And this morning, there were *two* gargoyles in his yard. Whatever is happening, it's happening at night. The only way to—"

"No!" Ashley interrupted sharply, shaking her head so hard that her blonde hair slapped her cheeks. "No way! I know what you're going to say and the answer is NO! *En-oh—NO!*"

"It's the only way to find out what's going on," I insisted. "We have to stay up. We have to stay up and keep an eye on his yard. We have to watch what happens. Tonight."

"But what if something really *is* going on?!?!" Ashley cried. "What if . . . what if the gargoyles really *are* real?"

"That's what we have to find out," I replied. "Are you with me?"

Ashley was quiet for a long time, then she looked at me.

"Do we have to go into Mr. Hansel's yard?" she asked.

"No," I answered, shaking my head. "We can stay out of his yard, in the bushes. I'll bring a flashlight. If something happens, we can run."

39

Ashley was quiet again. She clearly didn't like the idea.

"Come on," I urged. "We have to find out. Besides . . . we'll both be close to our homes. If something happens and we get into trouble, we can run. We'll be able to get away." I tried to sound as convincing as I could. I really wanted Ashley to come with me. I didn't want to be out alone at night, spying on Mr. Hansel's house all by myself.

But if I had to go alone, I would.

"All right," she said finally. "I'll go."

We agreed to meet at my house just before dark.

The nightmare was about to begin.

9

The rest of that day I just hung out around the house. Every once in a while I would look out my window or go outside, glancing over at Mr. Hansel's yard. The two gargoyles stood alone, facing the street. I guess I expected to see another gargoyle appear, but none did. And I didn't see anything of Mr. Hansel himself, either.

Which wasn't all that unusual. I don't think hardly anybody sees Mr. Hansel.

I searched to find out everything I could

about gargoyles. We have a bunch of books that had some stuff about them, but all it said was that gargoyles weren't real. I even hunted around on the internet. There was lots of stuff about gargoyles there, but once again, all I could find out was that they weren't real. They were just make believe. I couldn't find any information about anyone who had seen a 'real' gargoyle.

Maybe I had imagined everything last night. Maybe what I saw was just a big bat, or an owl.

But I didn't think so. I knew what I saw.

I saw a gargoyle.

A real one.

Ashley met me at my house just before night fell. She was wearing all dark clothes: dark jeans and a dark shirt, and she had her hair tied back in a ponytail. In her back pocket was a flashlight.

"I'm ready," she said.

I took a flashlight from the kitchen and told my Mom that I was going outside. Mom and Dad are pretty cool. In the summertime, they let me stay out late . . . as long as I stay close to home.

We went outside and waited. It wasn't quite dark yet, so we sat on the porch and talked about our plan.

"We'll go over to those bushes over there," I pointed. "No one will see us if we crouch down low. From there we'll be able to see Mr. Hansel's yard."

"But those bushes *are* in Mr. Hansel's yard," Ashley said.

"I know, but it's the only place that we'll be able to hide without being seen."

"I'm not so sure about this," Ashley said quietly.

"You're not backing out now, are you?" I asked sternly. I didn't say it to be mean. As it grew darker, even I was having second thoughts about this whole thing.

But then again, I really wanted to find out what was going on in Mr. Hansel's yard.

"No, I'm not backing out," Ashley answered. "I'm just . . . I don't know. I guess I'm a little afraid."

"Me too," I confessed. "But we'll be all right. I promise."

Night came, and it grew darker. The sounds of the city began to change. The hum of cars from the busy street on the next block began to fade. Every minute or so, we heard the high-pitched squeal of a bat as it darted through the sky in search of bugs. A nighthawk screeched high above. Most of the other kids that had been playing in their yards went inside. One by one, crickets began to chirp, and soon the air was filled with the soothing buzz of the unseen insects.

I looked at Ashley. "Ready?" I asked.

She drew a breath. "Ready," she said, standing up.

It only took a few seconds to slip across the dark yard and duck into the bushes. We tried to be as quiet as we could, not sure if anyone was watching us or not. It felt creepy being so close to Mr. Hansel's house like we were. If he found us, we'd sure be in a lot of trouble!

Even though it was dark, it was still lighter than it was last night. Tonight, the moon was out, and it cast an eerie glow over everything. The sky was dotted with millions of stars. And it was getting colder.

I don't know how long we sat there in the bushes, not saying anything. We waited and waited. Then we waited some more. We kept waiting.

Nothing. I began to think that we were wasting our time.

I was just about to tell Ashley that we'd

waited long enough, that nothing was going to happen tonight. I opened my mouth to speak — and it was then that I heard the flapping of wings.

The sound came from behind us, way up in the sky. Ashley and I could hear the heavy thumping of wings as they beat the air.

"Oh my gosh!" Ashley whispered. "You were right!"

"Of course I was right," I said, my eyes scanning the night sky. *"I told you I saw something last night. Something that flew. It looked like a gargoyle!"*

But right now, we couldn't see anything. It

was too dark, and whatever was making the flapping sound was still high in the sky.

"*Is it a gargoyle?*" Ashley whispered excitedly.

"*I don't know,*" I whispered back. "It's too dark to see anything."

We were still hunched low in the bushes, peering out between the branches. We could hear the flapping of wings, but it was impossible to see where the sound was coming from.

The only thing we knew was that whatever it was, it was getting closer!

"D-d-do gargoyles bite?" Ashley stammered.

"How should I know?" I answered back. "Gargoyles aren't even supposed to be real. They're just make-believe."

Ashley and I were frozen, huddled in our hiding place in the bushes. We turned our heads to scan the night sky, trying to see where the flapping was coming from.

"*There!*" Ashley suddenly hissed, pointing. "*Over there!*"

She was right! In the sky, there was a huge dark shadow! It looked just like the creature I had seen last night.

I knew that it was a gargoyle.

It swooped lower, gliding over the treetops

and flying in a big circle overhead.

"Is it a gargoyle?" Ashley asked again. She must have thought that I was an expert on gargoyles or something.

"It has to be," I replied. "There isn't anything else that could be that big. Not even an eagle."

We watched the shadow loop in the sky above us. It darted back and forth and all around, skimming over the treetops. Once, it flew beneath the street light and we were able to get a better look at it.

It sure looked like a gargoyle to me!

The creature soared back up into the night sky.

Suddenly it dove almost straight down! It was as fast as lightning. There was a great fluttering of wings as the creature came closer to the ground.

Closer . . . .

Closer . . . .

Suddenly, the flapping stopped. The shadow disappeared.

We sat in silence, listening. Where had the gargoyle gone? Had it flown off? Maybe it had landed in a tree. Or in the grass.

"I'm going to turn on my flashlight and look in the yard," I whispered.

"Are you crazy?!?!" Ashley asked in a hoarse whisper. "What if it's still around? What happens if it gets mad?"

Good question. I wasn't sure if I wanted to be face-to-face with a mad gargoyle.

I wasn't sure if I wanted to be face-to-face with a happy gargoyle, for that matter!

I was reaching for my flashlight when I heard a noise. Again, it was a fluttering of wings, but this time it was a lot closer.

"It's in the yard!" Ashley hissed. "It's right in front of us in the grass!"

We could hear movement in the yard, not twenty feet away from us. It was the muffled sound of shuffling, like someone—or *something*—was walking through the grass.

Then it stopped.

Ashley and I listened. We could still hear the steady chirping of crickets. A car horn blared twice in the distance, and the faint drone of a plane came from high in the sky.

But other than that—

Silence. All was quiet. But I knew that whatever had made the sound . . . whatever had landed in the yard . . . was still there.

I slowly drew out my flashlight, and Ashley

pulled hers out of her pocket.

"On the count of three," I said. "One . . ."

I raised my flashlight and pointed it through the bushes.

"Two . . . "

Ashley shifted on the ground, and placed her thumb on the flashlight button. She looked at me and nodded. She was ready.

"Three!"

We clicked on our flashlights.

The white beam pierced through the branches, scattering shadows all across the yard. In the middle of the yard stood a dark form, and I couldn't believe what I saw.

My jaw dropped. Ashley and I both gasped. A wave of terror swept through my entire body.

There was no mistake.

It was Mr. Hansel . . . and he looked *mad!*

Our flashlight beams were trained right on Mr. Hansel as he stood in the yard. The gargoyle statues were next to him. It was plain to see that we had surprised him, and he didn't look the least bit happy about it.

"Oh my gosh!" Ashley said. She didn't whisper, either. She said it loud and clear.

Mr. Hansel started walking towards us!

"Hey, you kids!" he sneered angrily. "I see you in those bushes! Come out now!"

"He sees us!" Ashley whispered, her voice quivering.

"No, he can't!" I whispered back. "He knows where we are, but the flashlights are blinding him. He knows *where* we are . . . but he doesn't know *who* we are!"

And it was true. As Mr. Hansel stormed toward us, he raised his arms to shield his eyes from the bright light.

I know that we should have jumped up and run away right then and there, but another movement caught my attention.

One of the cement gargoyles in the lawn had moved! I was sure of it! It looked like it fluttered its wings just a little bit. Then it was still again.

But then I noticed something else: There were now *three* gargoyles in the yard! Last night there had been one . . . then, this morning there had been two . . . *now there were three!*

Where were they coming from?

There was no time to think about it now. Mr. Hansel was getting closer with every second. His unkempt gray hair stood up on his head. He was taking big strides now. I'd never seen him move so fast before. He had always seemed to be such a feeble old man.

"We've got to get out of here!" Ashley cried.

She was right. Mr. Hansel was only a few steps away.

I snapped to my feet and bolted out from the bushes, followed closely by Ashley.

"Hurry!" she cried, urging me on.

"I'll get you!" Mr. Hansel shouted from behind us.

But I knew we were faster than he was.

At least, I sure hoped we were!

"Shut your light off!" I panted. "Otherwise, he'll be able to see where we are!" I clicked my flashlight off, and Ashley clicked hers off, too.

We ran alongside Mr. Hansel's house, along the high, wood fence around his back yard, and through another yard. It was hard going, because we had to keep our flashlights off. I kept hoping that I wouldn't run into something like Ashley had done last night.

When I thought we were a safe distance away, I stopped. Ashley bounded up next to me, her lungs heaving.

"I think we've lost him," I said, gasping for air.

"I hope so," Ashley said, falling to the ground. "I don't think I can run any more."

"Me neither," I heaved, tumbling to the grass. We listened closely for Mr. Hansel trudging after us. All we could hear were the normal sounds of nighttime in Gaylord. Cars in the distance, and a few crickets.

After a few minutes of rest, we were sure that Mr. Hansel wasn't after us. Maybe he had grown tired and went back home. Or maybe he just couldn't see very well in the dark.

Whatever the reason, I was glad that we had been able to get away!

"Did you see the gargoyles in the yard?" I asked Ashley as I stood up. Ashley stretched and stood up, too.

"Yeah," she answered. "That *totally* freaked me out. Where are they coming from?"

"I don't know," I answered. "Like I said, gargoyles aren't even supposed to be real. But I know what I saw last night. And there was *another* gargoyle in Mr. Hansel's yard tonight! It was probably the one we saw flying around. What I want to know is what was Mr. Hansel doing in the yard?"

"Beats me," Ashley replied.

We began to walk home through the darkened yards. It was hard to see, and the distant streetlights on the other side of the houses didn't give us much light. Huge shadows sprawled across the yards. I didn't dare turn on my flashlight, for fear that maybe Mr. Hansel was still out here somewhere, looking for us. The thought of that weird old man chasing us gave me the creeps.

"I wonder if—" Ashley started to say, but I interrupted her.

"*Ssshhhh!*" I said, raising a finger to my lips.

We stopped walking, and stood frozen motionless.

"Did you hear that?" I whispered quietly. So quiet that Ashley could hardly hear me. I could hardly hear myself!

"Hear what?" she whispered back.

Suddenly, the noise came again! It was a heavy flapping, the sound of pushing air! There were two shadows—two *enormous* shadows—swarming over us in the night sky! The sound of their wings was growing louder, and their dark shadows were growing larger!

Gargoyles! They were coming for us!

"RUN!" I shouted. "Run as fast as you can!"

Ashley and I both sprang, but it was too late. The gargoyles were already upon us, their giant wings covering the sky above.

"Ahhhh!" Ashley screamed. *"It's got me! IT'S GOT MEEEEEEEE!"* As she screamed, her voice suddenly sounded farther away. She was in the air!

Oh no! A gargoyle had captured Ashley! I could hear her screaming from the sky as the gargoyle carried her off!

"Help me Corky!" she screamed. *"Help*

meeeeeeee!"

This was all my fault. If I hadn't been the one who wanted to wait in Mr. Hansel's yard tonight, we wouldn't be in this mess. We'd be home watching TV or reading a book. Or babysitting my little brother.

Now, here we were only a few blocks from home, and Ashley has been kidnapped by a gargoyle—and it looked like I was going to be next!

But not if I could help it!

I dove to the cold grass and began to roll, just like I had done last night. My flashlight fell from my pocket, but I wasn't about to take the time to try and find it. I kept rolling and rolling, not knowing where I was headed. All I knew was that I wasn't going to stop.

Above, in the sky, I could hear the second gargoyle flapping its wings as it followed me over the dark yard. It swooped over me, and I suddenly felt a strong claw grab me by the shoulder. Then another claw grabbed my other shoulder.

"Let me go!" I screamed. *"Let me go, you slimly lizard with wings! Help! Help! Anybody!"*

But it was no use. The gargoyle was too strong. They had surprised us, and we hadn't even had the time to try and run away.

With one strong heave I was lifted off the

ground! I was being carried into the air, high into the night sky! I tried to scream, but I was so terrified, no sound would come out.

Below me, the ground kept falling farther and farther away. Actually, I couldn't see the ground, but I could tell from the lights of the houses that I was being carried way up into the sky. I could see the lights of downtown Gaylord, and cars driving on the streets. A long ways off, I saw the blinking red lights of a radio tower.

I was horrified. Worse! I was double-horrified.

Triple horrified! I have never been so scared in my whole life.

And what was worse, if the gargoyle let me go now, then I'd really be in trouble!

The creature's claws dug into my shoulder, clinging tightly. It really kind of hurt, but I couldn't do anything. The gargoyle had such a strong hold on me that I couldn't even move my arms.

It was hopeless. There was nothing I could do, except look at the city lights below me as I was lifted higher and higher into the night sky. There were hundreds of cars on the streets, and I'm sure that there were people out and about, going to movies and having fun—all completely unaware of what was happening in the sky above.

Gargoyles. Ashley and I had been captured by two huge gargoyles. Where were they taking us? What did they want us for?

I was about to find out . . . and never in a million years could I have guessed what was about to happen next.

Suddenly, we began to go back toward the ground again. At first, we started to descend very slowly, but soon, we were headed toward the ground very fast.

"Corky!" I heard Ashley shout. "Can you hear me?!?!?" It was hard to understand her over the loud flapping of wings. Her voice sounded like she was somewhere in front of me, but I couldn't be sure.

"I can *hear* you, but I can't *see* you!" I shouted back.

"I . . . I think we're going back to the ground!"

Question was, where were we going? Where were they taking us? I could still see the lights of downtown Gaylord. I didn't think we were too far from where we lived.

But wherever we were headed, we were sure going there in a hurry! The wind rushed past furiously, making my eyes water. I could make out streetlights and lights from houses. We were headed for the ground at a million miles an hour!

Either way you looked at it, I was sure we were goners. We were either going to be eaten by gargoyles . . . or hit the ground at a million miles an hour.

I didn't know which would be worse.

At the last second, I closed my eyes. I couldn't bear to watch.

Sharp talons tightened their grip around my shoulders. Wings beat the air heavily.

We were slowing down! At the very last instant, we were slowing. In the next moment, we landed safely on the ground. The gargoyle loosened his grip on my shoulders. He let me go! He let me go and then he flew off, back into the night sky.

"Ashley!" I shouted. "Where are you?!?!?"

"Over here!" she cried. I still couldn't see her, but I began walking in the direction of her voice.

"Keep talking so I can find where you are," I said.

"Over here! I'm over here!"

I followed the sound of her voice until I finally bumped into her.

"I can't believe that just happened!" she said.

"Me neither," I said. "We're lucky to be alive. Are you okay?"

"Yeah, I'm fine. But I lost my flashlight. And my shoulders hurt. Man, when my Dad finds out what that gargoyle did, he's really going to be in for it!"

"I lost my flashlight, too," I said. "But we've got to get home. Come on."

But then I noticed something very strange. As I looked around, no lights were on. There weren't any lights on anywhere. No street lights, no house lights, nothing.

I looked up. I could see stars in the sky, but all around us, it was very dark.

"Ashley . . . *look*. Look around. There's no lights anywhere."

Ashley was quiet for a moment, then she spoke.

"Well, maybe the power went out again, like it did last night," she said.

"Huh-uh," I responded, shaking my head in

the darkness. "When the gargoyles were flying, I could see the lights of the city. I'm sure the power is still on. But where are we?"

"I don't care," Ashley said. "I just want to go home."

"But which way do we go?" I asked. "It's so dark, I can't even see you. We might be in my back yard. Or yours, for that matter. We can't tell."

"Maybe if we just waited a few minutes until our eyes got used to the dark," Ashley said hopefully, "we could see better."

So we waited. I don't know how long we waited for, but I do know this: it was just as dark as it had always been. I couldn't see a thing.

"This is ridiculous," I said.

"Wait a minute!" Ashley said. "Listen!"

We listened for a few seconds.

"I don't hear anything," I said.

"Exactly," Ashley replied. "Nothing. No crickets, no cars, nothing. There's nothing to hear!"

I listened again, trying to detect even the faintest sound.

She was right! There was nothing to hear, except the shuffling of our own feet and our own breathing in the cool night air.

"Too weird," I said.

And for the very first time since the gargoyles

had let us go, I began to feel that something was really wrong. For whatever reason, the gargoyles had released us.

But where were we? At first, I thought that we were close to home. Now, it seemed like we were far, far away.

"We're not ever going to get home," Ashley pouted.

"Never get home," a voice suddenly hissed in the darkness.

We both jumped.

"Did you hear that?" I whispered.

"Yeah, I—" but Ashley was interrupted by the strange voice.

"Never get home," it hissed, and it began repeating itself. *"Never get home, never get home, never get home . . . ."*

"Where is it coming from?" I whispered.

"It's . . . it's coming from all around us!" Ashley stammered.

Then, other voices began to join in. *"Never get home, never get home, never get home . . . ."*

There were dozens of them, whatever they were.

"Never get home, never get home, never get—"

Not only were there dozens of them—but they were getting *closer!*

67

14

The hissing and chanting continued all around us, until it grew so loud that I threw my hands up over my ears. Ashley screamed, but I couldn't tell what she said, if anything at all.

Suddenly, the air was filled with the sound of flapping wings. They were all around us, and although I couldn't see them, I knew there had to be hundreds of them. And I was sure I knew what they were.

Gargoyles.

Some of them sounded so close that I had to

duck down. They all took flight at the same time, and the thunder of flapping wings was deafening. I was afraid that another gargoyle would grab me by the shoulders and try and haul me off. I wasn't going to let it happen this time!

Not if I could help it, anyway.

Thankfully, I didn't have to worry. Soon, all of the gargoyles had taken flight. Their wings beat the air high above, and the fluttering faded. Within a few seconds it was quiet again.

Just where in the world are we? I wondered. We still couldn't see a thing—not a single light, nothing. Only the stars in the sky above. And we couldn't hear anything. We were swallowed up once again by an eerie silence.

"How can this be?" Ashley wondered aloud. "How can we be so close to home and not hear or see anything? I mean . . . we went way up in the air when those gargoyles grabbed us . . . but I didn't think they took us that far."

"They didn't," I agreed. "Something's fishy, here. I don't know what it is, but something isn't right."

"Well, you got us into this mess," Ashley said, with anger in her voice. "What do we do now, Miss Gargoyle Hunter?"

Ashley was right. This was my fault. I was

the one who insisted that we hide in the bushes next to Mr. Hansel's house. Now we were lost . . . somewhere. We had to still be in Gaylord, I was sure . . . but then again, when we couldn't see or hear anything, we could be anywhere!

"I guess I don't know what to do," I admitted. "I didn't think we'd have a problem like this."

"Okay, let's think about this for a second," Ashley said. "We have to be close to home. I mean . . . the gargoyles took us high into the air, but they didn't take us very far from home. We have to be close to our houses."

"Wait a minute," I said. "I thought I recognized our street when the gargoyles brought us back to the ground. But I also recognized Mr. Hansel's house. We might be in his back yard."

"Maybe so, but we'd still see the lights of the city," I said. "And house lights. All of the houses on our street are fairly close together. We should be able to see a few house lights, no matter what back yard we're in."

"No, not necessarily," I responded. "Remember, Mr. Hansel has a high fence that goes all around his back yard. We wouldn't be able to see through it if we tried."

All of a sudden we heard another voice! It

71

was a strange, hissing sound, more than a whisper, but a voice nonetheless.

And it didn't sound human!

"Never get home," it said.

I froze. Ashley grabbed my arm.

"Never get home," the voice said again.

"Who . . . who's there?" I stammered.

"Never get home, never get home," the voice spoke again. Only this time, it sounded closer!

Ashley grabbed my arm tighter. What would we do? Was it a gargoyle? Was he going to hurt us?

"What do you want from us?" I managed to ask.

"Ahh, so many questionssss," the voice responded in the darkness. *"So many, many questionssss, yet so few answerssssss."*

"Listen here," I said, trying to sound brave. "When my Dad finds out what's going on, you're going to be in for it. You and all of your creepy gargoyle friends, or whatever you are."

The voice began to laugh! It was a coughing, throaty laugh, almost like he was choking. He spoke.

"That'sssss funny," the voice wheezed, still chuckling a bit. *"We don't get many laughsssss here in Darkland."*

"Huh?" I said. "Darkland? Where is

Darkland?"

"Why, it's where you are at this moment," the voice hissed. "It is where we all live. Darkland . . . the land of the gargoylesssss. And now, it's where you live. This is your home now . . . forever, and ever, and ever, and ever . . . . "

I did *not* like this. I did not like this at all.

It might have been a little easier if we could see, but we were in total darkness. Everything was completely black. I knew that Ashley was by my side, only a few inches away . . . but I couldn't see her.

Maybe that's why it was called Darkland.

"Are . . . are you going to hurt us?" Ashley asked. Her voice trembled as she spoke.

"Me? No, not at all, not at all," the strange voice replied. *"Certainly not I."*

"What is 'Darkland'?" I asked. So far, all I knew about Darkland was that it was very dark. And gargoyles lived here.

"Darkland is very, very old," the voice replied, in a voice just above a whisper. *"It has existed longer than time. It has always, and always will, exist. It is where all gargoyles are destined to live."*

"Who?" I asked. "Who are *you*?"

"We are the Gargoyles of Darkland, of course. This is our home."

Maybe Ashley was getting braver, or maybe she wasn't believing the voice that spoke to us in the darkness, because she suddenly blurted out in a loud voice: *"GARGOYLES AREN'T REAL!"*

Her voice echoed through the darkness, and faded away. Then:

Silence. There was nothing but the silence of the darkness, the silence of . . . .

Darkland.

"Yessssss, we are real," the voice answered slowly. *"We are as real as you are. Darkland is real . . . and we are real."*

"Then how did *we* get here?" I asked angrily. Then, before the voice could respond, I answered my own question: "I'll tell you how! Gargoyles grabbed us and brought us here. How do you explain that?!?!?" I was really getting mad.

76

"*Of course they did,*" the voice answered. "*They captured you in your world and brought you to our world. It's your own fault, I'm afraid.*"

"Our *own* fault?!?!?" I replied, my voice rising. "What do you mean it was our 'own fault'?!?! We didn't do anything wrong!"

"*You didn't have to do anything wrong,*" the voice answered. "*You were just in the wrong place at the wrong time.*"

"All we were doing was trying to find out where the cement gargoyles were coming from," Ashley offered. "We weren't doing anything wrong. I mean . . . come on. Cement gargoyles aren't even real."

"*Oh, but they are, they are,*" the voice hissed quietly. "*But you'll know all about them soon enough.*"

What did he mean by that? Were we going to meet up with more gargoyles? What was going to happen?

I was about to ask, but I didn't have to. The voice continued.

"*You'll know, soon enough. Soon enough, you'll be just like us. Soon enough, you too, will be a gargoyle. You will be one of us, living in Darkland, forever and ever and ever.*"

I screamed. Ashley screamed. We screamed and screamed, hoping that somehow, someone would hear us. We thought that maybe, some how, some way, someone would come and save us.

No one did.

We were alone.

Alone in Darkland.

With hundreds . . . thousands . . . maybe even millions . . . of gargoyles.

I was wrong. We *weren't* alone.

Of course, there were all of the gargoyles that lived in Darkland. They were around somewhere. I had no idea where they had gone, but they couldn't be too far away.

But all of a sudden a light appeared! It looked like a flashlight, sweeping back and forth! Maybe someone was coming to save us! Maybe Dad was looking for us!

But, then again, maybe not. Because the voice I heard next was certainly *not* my Dad's.

"I know you're here!" a gruff voice spoke angrily.

Mr. Hansel!

How did *he* get here?!?!?

Actually, when I thought about it, he was probably their king. He was probably the King of the Gargoyles.

Well, maybe not.

"You're hear somewhere!" he bellowed, only this time he was a lot closer.

"Run!" Ashley shouted, and I heard her feet pound the ground. I took flight as well, following the sound of Ashley's pounding footsteps.

This was dangerous. We were running in total blackness, unable to see where we were going.

Behind us, I could still hear Mr. Hansel shouting, but he sounded a lot farther away.

"NO!" he was screaming. "YOU MUSTN'T RUN! DON'T RUN!"

Suddenly, Ashley screamed! Her voice was loud and then it quickly faded away. When I realized what had happened it was too late. The unthinkable had happened.

Ashley had fallen! Not only that, but I could hear her voice as it plummeted down a deep canyon.

She had fallen off a cliff!

I tried to stop running before I fell, too, but it was a little too late for that. The ground suddenly fell away, and there was nothing beneath my feet. Wind rushed past my face as I tumbled through the air.

This was it! Ashley and I were goners!

17

I could hear Ashley's frantic screaming below me as she continued to fall. Warm air rushed past as we continued falling, faster and faster. I closed my eyes.

We fell for a few more moments, and I got brave and opened up one eye just a little bit.

Something was happening as we fell faster and faster downward.

I opened both eyes.

Slowly . . . very slowly . . . the darkness faded away. It seemed the farther we fell, the lighter it became! The darkness was giving way to a strange, yellow glow, like daylight. I could actually see Ashley below me as she fell.

And I could also see something else.

Water. We were falling toward a lake of some sort! It was racing toward us, and there was nothing we could do!

I wished I wouldn't have opened my eyes!

By now Ashley had stopped screaming. I think she probably was trying, but she had already screamed her lungs out. I was too horrified to scream. I knew that if I tried, not a single sound would come out.

Below us, the water was quickly approaching, faster, faster still. In a few seconds, we would hit.

Oh, how I wish I was home in bed! Or curled up on the couch with a good book in my own living room, in my own home!

I caught a movement out of the corner of my eye and turned my head.

Now I DID scream!

It was a gargoyle! The biggest gargoyle I had ever seen! Of course, I haven't seen a lot of gargoyles, but this one was huge—and he was coming right at me! It was horrible! I was either going to hit the ground at a billion miles an hour, or I was going to be eaten by a gargoyle!

Below me, another gargoyle appeared in the sky. He was going for Ashley! We were going to be meal deals for gargoyles!

The gargoyle swooped down and around, and dove. It tried to grab Ashley, but it missed.

I suddenly thought about how strange my life had become. Not more than an hour ago, I had been at home in Gaylord, safe and sound. Now I was in Darkland, home of the gargoyles.

Some things are just too strange to understand.

The gargoyle that tried to catch me suddenly flew right under me! He tried to grab my legs but I kicked and twisted away from him. I could see his sharp claws as he reached up to grab me, and I twisted just in time before a razor-sharp talon would have caught me in the arm.

But now we had another problem.

We were going to hit the water. We were going to hit the water and there was nothing we could do about it.

I could see the shimmering blue surface below, coming at me faster, faster still . . . .

This was it! We were done for!

18

Ashley was first. I heard her scream a moment before she hit the surface, and then her shout was drowned out by the explosion of spraying water. She disappeared beneath the waves.

I was next!

I took the deepest breath I could and held it.

SPLASH! I hit the water!

Suddenly, I didn't know which way was up or down! The water was cold, but I hardly noticed it. I was too worried about making it back to the surface . . . before I ran out of air.

I opened my eyes.

The surface! I could see the surface above me, through millions of tiny, swirling bubbles. I spread out my arms, kicked my legs, and began to propel myself upward.

Could I make it before I ran out of air?

I had to. I just *had* to.

I kept kicking and swimming in an effort to make it to the surface. I'm a good swimmer, but I had plunged far below the surface . . . farther than I had ever been before.

I could feel my chest begin to hurt as my lungs cried out for air. But I had to keep moving! If I could make it just a few more feet . . . just a bit farther . . . .

Sploosh!

I made it!

I gasped loudly, and took a deep breath, let it out, then took another. I felt dizzy.

That had been a close one. We had fallen a long ways and hit the water pretty hard. I could have drowned!

I coughed and sputtered and snapped my head around. My hair dripped down in front of my face, and I wiped it away. I coughed once more, treading water in this very strange, strange place.

But something was wrong.

Ashley!
She was gone!

19

"ASHLEY!" I shouted. My voice echoed out over the water. "Ashley! Where are you?!?!?"

I became more and more worried. Where was Ashley? Had she drowned? Was she gone?!?!? I was terrified.

I was about to dive below the surface, to go look for her, when all of a sudden her head popped up! The water exploded and she splashed to the surface, flailing her arms and snapping her head back. She coughed and sputtered, and took a deep breath. I swam over to her.

"Are you all right?" I asked, helping her to stay afloat.

"I . . . I think so," she said, in between coughs. "Yeah . . . I think I'm okay."

"Me too," I said. "We were really lucky. We fell a long way down here."

I looked around. The sky above was very strange. It was a dark, misty gray, but there were no clouds. Far in the distance, I could see tall mountains and thick forests. Directly in front of us, stretching high into the sky, was a rock ledge.

"That's where we fell from," I said, looking up.

"Where is this place?" Ashley asked. "We were in total darkness . . . but as we fell down, it became lighter. This is freaky."

But I didn't have an answer for her. My only guess was that we were somewhere in Darkland.

"Come on," I said, bringing my arm up over my head and splashing forward. I began crawling through the water toward the rock wall. Not far from the wall, it gave way to a rocky shoreline. We would be able to get out of the water there. Ashley followed, and in a few seconds we stood on the shore, dripping wet.

Again, we looked at our surroundings. It was the strangest place I had ever seen. There was no sun, and everything looked on the verge of twilight. It looked just like it would if it were early morning or late evening. It was unbelievable, and yet I knew that somehow, all of this was actually happening. I know when I dreaming, because I can usually wake myself up.

I didn't even try to this time.

I knew I wasn't dreaming. I knew what was happening simply couldn't be real, but it was.

"Corky! Look!" Ashley's hand suddenly shot up into the air. I looked up to see what she was pointing at.

Far above us, wheeling in the sky, were two gargoyles. They were huge! Their wings pumped slowly, like super-giant geese.

Super-giant geese with claws and teeth, that is.

"Those must have been the ones that tried to catch us in the air," Ashley said quietly.

"Quick!" I said. "Let's find someplace to hide! They might still be looking for us!"

We ran up the shore to where a line of trees began, ducking under the thick canopy of branches. We were safe . . . at least for the time being.

"Can you still see the gargoyles?" Ashley asked, peering up through the branches.

"No," I whispered, shaking my head. The

sky was empty.

But a movement near the rock wall caught my attention.

There was something there! I could see something moving, hiding in a crack in the rock wall . . . and now it was coming out!

20

I gasped and held my breath. Whatever it was, it wasn't very far away. If it was a gargoyle, there would be no place for us to run! We'd be caught for sure!

Suddenly, the creature came into view — but it wasn't a creature at all! It was —

Mr. Hansel!

It was Mr. Hansel, and boy — did he look mad!

Maybe that was it. Maybe Mr. Hansel *was* the King of the Gargoyles, after all. Maybe he was their leader.

We were goners now, for sure. All of the terrible stories I'd heard about Mr. Hansel *were* true, after all.

Ashley and I huddled close.

"What do we do now?" she whispered.

"I don't know," I whispered back. I thought about running, but to where? I had no idea where to go. Besides . . . if we just took off and started running, there was a chance that we'd be spotted by a gargoyle. I did *not* want to go for another free ride in the clutches of a flying reptile!

We were prisoners.

Prisoners in Darkland.

And what was worse, mean Mr. Hansel was here. He spotted us beneath the tree and stormed over to us.

"Why didn't you listen to me?!?!" he demanded. But Ashley and I were so frightened that we couldn't speak.

"Why didn't you listen to me?!?!?" he asked again, even louder. His eyebrows scrunched together, and his eyes looked scary and mean. His cheeks were drawn tight, and his gray hair was all messy as usual.

"We were afraid," I managed to answer.

"Afraid?!?! Afraid of what?!?! Of *me?!?!*"

All I could do was nod my head.

"You shouldn't be here," Mr. Hansel said. "You shouldn't be here at all. Darkland isn't for children. It's too dangerous."

"Well, what are *you* doing here?" Ashley asked.

"I am the Gatewatcher of Darkland," he replied, very matter-of-factly. When he didn't offer any further explanation, I spoke.

"What does the Gatewatcher do? And just what is this 'Darkland'? All we know about it is that gargoyles live here."

"Darkland is the eternal realm of gargoyles," he answered, shaking his head. "No humans should be here, especially children."

"You're here," I said. "You're a human. Unless you turn into a gargoyle or something."

At this, Mr. Hansel's eyes grew wide, and he burst into a fit of laughter. I didn't think it was so funny, but he sure did.

"Me?!?!" he said, finally getting a hold of himself. "A gargoyle?!?! I hardly think so. I am merely the Gatewatcher."

There was that word again.

Gatewatcher.

"Just what does the 'Gatewatcher' do?" I asked.

"The Gatewatcher must always be on the lookout for gargoyles that try and escape into the real world. Someone must mind the gate, to make certain that gargoyles do not get out."

I was starting to ease a bit. I didn't think that Mr. Hansel was going to hurt us, and I relaxed.

But this whole new world was very puzzling. What did it exist for? And why do the gargoyles have to have a 'Gatewatcher' to keep them in Darkland?

I had so many questions, but I didn't know where to start.

"You see," Mr. Hansel continued, "last week, one of the gargoyles from Darkland escaped. He entered the real world. Gargoyles have special powers, but mainly, they have the power to turn to stone. That's how they can hide so well."

"But we saw *three* gargoyles in your yard today," I said.

"Ah, yes," the old man replied. "That's another problem. Not only can gargoyles turn themselves to stone, they also have the power to make stone gargoyles come alive."

A lump the size of an apple formed in my throat and stuck there.

"What . . . what do they do once they come alive?" Ashley asked.

Mr. Hansel didn't answer. He had a very worried look on his face, and he stared at the ground. Finally, he looked at us.

"Once the stone gargoyles are brought to life, they comb the city in search of children. They find children, and then they bring them here. To Darkland. You are the first two. Even at this moment, there are gargoyles in Gaylord, looking for children, waiting for the right moment to snatch them up and bring them here."

My whole body trembled. This was crazy! Gargoyles . . . especially *stone* gargoyles . . . aren't real!

They're not supposed to be, anyway.

But it was all beginning to make sense. The gargoyle in Mr. Hansel's yard that Ashley had tripped over last night had been real, after all. And the ones we saw this morning, including the ones who had kidnapped us and brought us here to Darkland.

"But why do they want us here?" I asked. "What is going to happen to us?"

Again, Mr. Hansel looked very concerned. The lines of his face were deep and troubled, and his eyes became sad.

"You have been brought here to become one of them," he said grimly. "That is why they brought you here. To turn you into gargoyles."

Oh no! Gargoyles?!?!? Ashley and I were going to turn into gargoyles?!?!?

I thought I was going to faint.

Suddenly, we heard the sound of flapping wings in the distance. Mr. Hansel turned his head to the sky, and my eyes followed his gaze.

"They're coming!" he suddenly cried. "Quick! You can still get away, but there is no time to waste! This way! Quickly!" He spun and began to run, and Ashley and I sprang and followed him.

In the next instant the air was filled with hundreds of gargoyles! Their wings beat the air like a herd of thundering elephants!

They were the gargoyles of Darkland . . . and they were coming for us!

21

Our feet pounded the ground, but the only thing we could hear were the beating of wings in the sky above. I turned to catch a quick glance behind us, and instantly I wished I hadn't.

Gargoyles! Hundreds of them! They filled the sky like a cloud, coming closer and closer by the second.

"Hurry!" Mr Hansel shouted as we ran. But I was already running as fast as I could. So was Ashley.

"This way!" Mr. Hansel shouted. "We can

escape over here! Follow me!"

He didn't have to tell me twice!

We ran to the stone wall where Mr. Hansel had appeared. "Over here!" he shouted as he ran. For an old guy, he sure could run fast!

Suddenly, he stopped . . . and opened a door! There was a large wooden door set right in the side of the stone wall!

Mr. Hansel flung the door open and bolted inside, followed by Ashley, then me. He snapped the door closed and it banged shut.

"Made it," he said, securing the bolt on the door.

Outside, I could hear the thundering of wings as the gargoyles reached the door. It sounded like there were thousands of them!

Mr. Hansel wasted no time. He clicked on his flashlight and began walking down a thin hallway. Jagged stones stuck out from the sides. The rocks were wet, and they glistened in the beam of the flashlight. The air was cold and damp and stale.

"Where are we going?" Ashley asked. Her voice echoed down the strange, stone corridor.

"You'll see," Mr. Hansel answered. "You'll see."

We walked and walked, and the farther we went, the thinner the cave became. Soon, it was just barely wide enough to walk through. I scraped my elbows and shoulders on the wet rocks, and so did Ashley. Mr. Hansel was bigger than we were, so he had to walk sideways!

Suddenly he stopped. He reached his arms up and grabbed onto something. Mr. Hansel had opened up some kind of door in the ceiling of the stone tunnel. There was a wooden ladder there, and he climbed up.

Ashley was next, and I followed on her heels.

We climbed out and just stared. I couldn't believe what I was seeing!

It was a yard! We were in a normal, everyday yard! It was dark, and we couldn't see much, but I could smell the fresh air and hear the chirping of crickets. Stars dotted the sky above.

"What in the world?" Ashley gasped as we looked around. It was strange. "Where are we?" she asked.

"You are in my back yard," Mr. Hansel replied. As he spoke, he shined the flashlight over the yard, and I could see the tall wood fence.

He was right! We were in his back yard!

This was too weird. First, gargoyles kidnap us and take us to some place called 'Darkland', and then we escape though a long tunnel . . . and wind up in Mr. Hansel's back yard!

"Wait a minute," I said. "If we had to escape from Darkland through a tunnel, how did we get there in the first place? I mean . . . I don't remember going through any tunnel."

"I'll show you," Mr. Hansel said. He pointed the flashlight beam in another direction, and began to walk. Ashley and I followed.

He stopped.

"Be careful," he said. He pointed the flashlight beam by his feet.

We were at a ledge! Right where we stood, at our feet, the ground fell away! There was no more grass, nothing. It was just—

Dark.

"That's how they go back," Mr. Hansel said. "This is how the gargoyles enter Darkland."

We just stared. The flashlight beam swept through the darkness below us, but there was nothing to see. Nothing but pitch blackness.

"Is this why you built the fence?" I asked.

"Yes," Mr. Hansel answered. "When I first moved here years ago, it was just a normal yard. Then, one night, this big hole just opened up.

Shortly after that, I began to see the gargoyles. They were coming out of the hole over there—" He pointed the flashlight beam at the hole we had came out of. "And they would return by flying into the dark hole over here." Again, he shined the light over the ledge before us.

"But why do they have to climb out through the tunnel?" Ashley asked. "Can't they just fly back out of the big hole?"

"I thought so," Mr. Hansel replied. "But they can't. I don't know why. All I know is that they escape through the tunnel, and the only way they can return to Darkland is to fly back over this ledge. In this yard, it is always dark. Even during the day. You probably noticed that as you fell toward the water, things became lighter and lighter. That's how Darkland hides. Darkland hides from the rest of the world by remaining dark up here . . . but light down below. Darkland exists within the earth . . . below the earth's surface."

My gaze followed the flashlight beam as it swept across the depths of the enormous valley below us. But there was nothing to see. It was strange, knowing that far below in the darkness, was another world.

A world of gargoyles.

"I made that big door to cover the tunnel,"

Mr. Hansel explained. "But some gargoyles still manage to escape."

"So that's why you called yourself a 'gatewatcher'," I said.

"Yes," Mr. Hansel replied. "There have been gatewatchers like me for as long as Darkland has existed. Our job is to keep the gargoyles from escaping. Unfortunately, I haven't done a very good job."

"But what happens now?" I asked. "If there are real gargoyles in Gaylord, isn't everyone in danger?"

Mr. Hansel nodded sadly. "The only way we can stop them is by finding them during the day. If the gargoyles do not return to Darkland during the night, they turn to stone. They turn to stone when the sun is shining, and wait for darkness once again. We must find them, bring them here, and throw them over the ledge. Over the ledge, and back into Darkland."

"That's silly," Ashley said. "I mean . . . how can you tell if a gargoyle is real or not? Lots of people in Gaylord have stone gargoyles in their yards."

"If you look closely," Mr. Hansel answered, "real gargoyles will turn to stone during the day—that is, of course, except for their tongue.

Their entire body will be stone, but their tongue will be *real*."

And that's how our quest began. Oh, I didn't know it at the time, but everyone in Gaylord was in serious danger . . . and it was up to Ashley and I to stop the gargoyles of Darkland. We would have to hunt all over to find the real creatures and bring them back here, which wouldn't be easy. It wouldn't be easy, but there was no other way.

Our hunt for gargoyles was about to begin.

23

I didn't sleep very well that night. I kept tossing and turning, and every time I fell asleep, I was haunted by nightmares. In my dreams, huge gargoyles were chasing me. They would pick me up and carry me off to Darkland. I would run away, but they would pick me up and bring me back to their world again.

I got up early in the morning, ate some corn flakes for breakfast, and met Ashley in front of her house. The sky was baby blue, and only a few white puffy clouds could be seen. The sun was just beginning to rise through the trees. Birds were singing, and the air was fresh and clear.

And there were gargoyles in Mr. Hansel's yard. I could see them from our living room window, perched like statues in Mr. Hansel's front yard.

Only today there were four of them!

I walked over to Ashley's house, crossing the street in front of Mr. Hansel's. I knew that the gargoyles were made of cement, but I also knew that they were real. I didn't want to take any chances.

Ashley was waiting for me, and together we walked across the yard to Mr. Hansel's, keeping an eye on the four gargoyles in his front yard. Our plan was to meet up with Mr. Hansel, and the three of us would spread out and search Gaylord for more 'real' gargoyles.

We knocked on Mr. Hansel's door and waited.

And waited.

We waited some more. Ashley knocked again.

"Where could he be?" I wondered aloud.

We stood patiently at the door, but still no Mr. Hansel. We could hear no sounds coming from inside his house.

"Let's go around back and see if we can get

into his back yard," Ashley said.

We stepped off his porch and ran to the side of the house. The tall fence loomed before us, and we walked along side of it. I spotted a knot-hole, and stopped, leaning over to peer through the quarter-size hole.

"See anything?" Ashley asked.

"Nothing at all," I said, shaking my head. "It's just like Mr. Hansel said. It's all dark in there."

"How are we supposed to gather up the stone gargoyles and bring them back to Darkland if we can't get through the fence?" Ashley asked.

It was a good question. I guess we had counted on Mr. Hansel to help us out . . . but so far, there was no sign of him. It was like he had disappeared.

"Maybe the gargoyles got him," I said. "Maybe something's happened to him. Something terrible."

"Don't talk like that," Ashley said. "It gives me the creeps." We started walking along the fence again.

"Well, creeps or no creeps," I said, "we've got to start searching for gargoyles. You heard what Mr. Hansel said. At night, the real ones come alive and search for kids. We have to stop them. And we can start with the four that are in Mr. Hansel's yard."

"Hey, look!" Ashley suddenly said, pointing. Her attention was drawn to a board that had come loose in the fence. "I'll bet we could pull that back and get in from here," she said.

We both grabbed the board and began to pull. It was a struggle, but finally, the board gave way. It snapped and came loose, and we let it fall to the grass.

And inside was the strangest sight I had ever seen.

Mr. Hansel was right. His back yard was almost entirely dark. All around us was sunny and clear. The sun was now almost up over the trees, and the sky was blue and clear.

But looking through the fence where we had pulled the board away, the entire yard was very dark. It looked like it was night time.

But only in Mr. Hansel's back yard —
Only in Darkland.

"Come on," I said to Ashley, and I took a step through the fence.

"W-w-what are you d-d-doing?!?!?" Ashley stammered. I turned to face her.

"We have to go look," I said. "Maybe Mr. Hansel is back here. Besides . . . after we find the stone gargoyles, we'll have to bring them to Darkland anyway. Come on."

It was plain to see that Ashley didn't like the idea one bit. I didn't either, when it came right down to it. It was dangerous. The whole plan was daring and unbelievable. I guess we would be okay during the day when the gargoyles had all turned to stone.

But then again . . . .

Either way, we didn't have a choice in the matter.

I took another step, and stopped. Ashley followed me through the gaping hole in the fence.

The blue sky was suddenly gone. The sun was gone. Even the chirping birds were gone. Everything around us was dark and gloomy. We could make out a few things, like a tree and the grass. And we could see the back of Mr. Hansel's house. But everything was very dark, like it was night time—in early morning! It sure was crazy.

We walked over to the edge of the deep, black canyon of Darkland. There was nothing to see except inky black. I remembered that just last night we had fallen down there. How terrible! We were really lucky that there was water below us. If there hadn't been . . . .

Well, I tried not to think about that.

I turned and looked around the yard. I hadn't thought to bring a flashlight. I didn't think I would need one during the day! But I sure could have used one here in Mr. Hansel's back yard.

"I wonder where Mr. Hansel is," Ashley said.

"I don't know," I said. "But we're going to have to start without him. Are you ready?"

Ashley drew a deep breath. "I guess so," she said.

"Let's start with the gargoyles that are in Mr. Hansel's front yard," I said. Without another word, we walked over to the fence and slipped back through. Instantly we were in sunlight once again, and the morning was clean and bright. We walked around Mr. Hansel's house and saw the four gargoyles sitting in the front yard.

"Come on," I said, and we walked slowly, approaching the gargoyles with caution. When we were a few feet away from them, Ashley stopped.

"I'm scared," she said.

"Me too," I said, turning to face her for a moment. I turned back and looked at the gargoyles. "But you heard what Mr. Hansel said. During the day, the gargoyles are harmless. They can't hurt us."

"Yeah, but still —" Ashley said, not finishing her sentence. She got brave and took a few steps, and we both crept the last few feet.

We were standing right in front of the gargoyles.

They looked ugly and mean, and their huge, bug-eyes seemed to glare at us. Their claws were sharp and pointed, and I shivered when I remembered that Ashley and I had both been captured and carried high into the air. We were very lucky that we had been able to escape Darkland.

All of a sudden Ashley drew a deep breath, and her hand flew up to cover her mouth.

"Corky, look," she whispered. I looked closer at the gargoyle.

Mr. Hansel had been right. The gargoyles had turned to stone, all right . . . all except for their tongues.

All of their tongues were *real*.

25

It was the freakiest thing I have ever seen in my life. The entire gargoyle was made of a gray colored stone . . . but inside its mouth was a real tongue! It looked just like you would think a gargoyle's tongue would look like. It was pink and long.

And it moved! It seemed to slowly wag back and forth. The creature itself was completely motionless, but its tongue was very much alive, just like Mr. Hansel said. Ashley shuddered and took a step back. I did the opposite. I took a step forward, closer to the gargoyle.

I reached my hand out, and touched its arm.

There was no surprise, no shock, nothing. It was made of stone. Cold, gray stone. Cement.

"Come on," I said to Ashley. "Help me lift it."

"What?!?!" Ashley cried. "We can't lift that thing! It weighs a billion-jillion pounds, I bet."

"Well, we won't know until we try. Come on."

Reluctantly, Ashley took a step forward. I wrapped my arms around the gargoyle, and Ashley stepped to the other side of the creature and placed one hand under its arm.

"On three," I said. "One . . . two . . . three."

I drew a deep breath and heaved. Ashley heaved. We heaved so hard we almost fell flat on our backs.

But most amazing of all . . . we picked up the gargoyle! It didn't hardly weigh anything at all! The creature was very easy to lift.

"Wow!" I said, after regaining my balance. "This is easy."

"I thought he would have weighed a lot more," Ashley said.

"So did I," I replied. "Come on. Let's take it into Mr. Hansel's back yard."

Together, we carried the huge creature across

the yard. I was really nervous, thinking that at any moment, the creature might come alive and grab me.

I also wondered if it knew what was going on right now. Was it aware that we were carrying it back to Darkland? Was it sort of awake, but powerless to do anything? I had no idea.

Besides . . . right now, I was more concerned with getting the gargoyle through the fence and into Mr. Hansel's back yard.

Back to Darkland.

"Careful," Ashley said as we approached the fence.

It took a bit of squirming, but we were able to carry the gargoyle through the fence. Once again, we were in darkness. We could see a little bit, but we went slow.

"Okay," I told Ashley. "We're almost at the ledge."

We stopped.

"Ready?" I asked.

"Yep," Ashley answered, and with that, we heaved the gargoyle into the darkness over the ledge.

Suddenly the air below the ledge was filled with the sound of flapping wings! A loud screech echoed through the darkness.

The gargoyle had come alive! Ashley and I stood near the ledge, too afraid to even move. We could see his dark shape swooping in the air just below the ledge. It looked like it was trying to fly higher, to fly above the ledge, but it couldn't. After a few turns, it spun downward, into the darkness and out of sight.

It worked!

"One down, more to go," Ashley said.

"Yeah," I agreed. "Come on. Let's get those other three."

We turned and began to walk toward the fence . . . but stopped cold.

There was a noise coming from the tunnel! The same tunnel that we had used to escape Darkland . . . the same tunnel that the gargoyles had been using to escape! There was a noise coming from the tunnel . . . and now the door was opening up!

26

We froze. There wasn't time to run, and even if we did, we wouldn't have made it to the fence in time. I've seen gargoyles move . . . and they're fast!

Suddenly, the door burst open.

Mr Hansel! At the sight of us he jumped, and his eyes about popped out of his head. He instantly relaxed.

"What are you doing here?" he asked, climbing up out of the tunnel.

"We were looking for you," I replied. "We knocked on the door of your house but you weren't home. We've already brought one of the gargoyles back to Darkland."

"Good," he said, closing the door to the tunnel. Then he closed a latch and it made a loud clicking sound.

"That ought to do it," he said.

"What were you doing down there?" Ashley asked.

"I went down the tunnel all the way to the opening. I double-bolted the door from the inside, and I put this new latch on this door just this morning. Let's just say we won't have a problem with the gargoyles escaping."

I was relieved to hear him say that, but we still had a big problem: there were still gargoyles all over Gaylord. True, most of them were only stone statues, but some of them were *real*. Some of them were stone during the day, but would come alive at night. They came alive at night, searching for children to bring back to Darkland.

We had to stop them. We just *had* to.

"Let's get started," Mr. Hansel said, and then he noticed the fence where we had pulled the board away.

"Sorry," I offered, "but it was the only way we could get into your back yard. The board was already loose."

Mr. Hansel shrugged it off. "No bother," he said. "But there's a gate over here. It's a little easier."

We followed him across the dark yard and when we reached the fence he reached out, lifted a wood latch, and swung open a gate. He stepped back and let us through, and, once again, we were standing in bright sunshine.

Too weird.

Mr. Hansel closed the fence behind him.

"How are we going to find the gargoyles that are real?" Ashley wondered aloud. "They could be anywhere."

"Yes, they could be," Mr. Hansel said. "But they usually stick together. There's three left in my yard, and I think there might be a few more somewhere around Gaylord."

"Somewhere around Gaylord?!?!?" I asked. "We'll never be able to find them all before tonight!"

Mr. Hansel looked grim. "True," he said. "But we have to try. Let's get these three in the yard, and then we'll split up and look for more."

Suddenly I felt very silly. For as long as I could remember, I had always thought that Mr. Hansel was just a weird old man. Just because everyone had told me that he was strange, I just believed it. Sure, he might look a little odd, but now that I knew him better, it was plain to see that he was just a normal, average man.

With messy gray hair, of course.

It didn't take us long to carry the three gargoyles into his back yard. They looked very heavy, but actually they were pretty light. Mr. Hansel could even carry one all by himself. When we tossed them over the ledge, they suddenly came alive, flying about just below us. It looked like they were trying to fly above the ledge, but for some strange reason, they couldn't. Soon, they just disappeared into the darkness.

"Okay," Mr. Hansel said after the last gargoyle had been returned to Darkland. "Time for the real work to start."

The hunt was on, and the real work was about to begin.

Ashley and I had no idea where to begin. The gargoyles could be anywhere.

"The creatures like to stay together," Mr. Hansel assured us. "They feel safe when they're together. That's why I don't think that they spread out all over the place. I think all of the gargoyles — the real ones, anyway — will be within a few blocks from here."

"How many do you think there are?" Ashley asked.

"I'm not sure," Mr. Hansel said, shaking his

head. "Probably not many. But just one is too many. Just one gargoyle has the power to bring stone gargoyles to life just by touching them. If we miss one, then he can make other gargoyles come to life, and in turn, those gargoyles can bring others to life. If we don't get them all today, there might be dozens more by tomorrow."

Ashley and I were silent. I couldn't imagine dozens of gargoyles sweeping over the skies of Gaylord, searching for children.

We split up, each of us taking a street. Our plan was to scour the yards and search for real gargoyles . . . the ones with real tongues. When we found one, we would find each other and bring the gargoyle back to Darkland. I know it sounds crazy, but that's what we were doing.

I thought that I might even write a book about it, someday.

As luck would have it, I was the first one to find a real gargoyle.

It was in the front yard of a house, not too far from where I live. I had never seen the gargoyle there before. It was perched on the lawn near a shrub, and it was small. It only came up to my knees. On a closer inspection, I saw what I had been looking for:

A real tongue. Eeeww.

I looked around, up and down the street, but I didn't see any sign of Mr. Hansel or Ashley. I decided that, since the gargoyle was so small, I could take care of him myself.

I reached down and picked up the gargoyle by the wings. He was light and very easy to lift.

Suddenly, someone was shouting at me!

"Hey!" I heard a loud voice shout. *"Just what do you think you're doing?!?!?"*

I spun.

On the porch of the house stood a woman. The front door was open and she was glaring at me, and I realized something that I hadn't thought about: I was in her yard, taking something! She probably thought I was stealing! I was going to wind up in jail!

Think, Corky. Think.

I had no idea what to say. I was caught.

"So, it's *you*," the woman hissed angrily.

"Please . . . I can explain. Really."

"You don't need to explain," she said, stepping onto the porch and closing the screen door behind her. "I can see what you're up to. You're the one that's been putting those gargoyles in people's yards."

Huh? What did she mean by that?

"Well listen here, young lady. If I catch you

putting gargoyles in my yard again, I'm calling your parents. Understand?"

I sure did! Now I knew what she was talking about. She wasn't mad at me for *taking* the gargoyle . . . she was mad because she thought I was the one placing gargoyles in her yard!

"Yes, ma'am," I answered as politely as possible.

"Good," she replied, and stormed back in the house, closing the door behind her.

That had been a close one!

I walked quickly out of her yard and caught up with Ashley on the next block. I told her what happened.

"We're going to have to be real careful," Ashey said, "or we're going to get into a lot of trouble."

I nodded my head in agreement. "Come on," I said. "Let's get rid of this gargoyle and keep looking."

We took the gargoyle into Mr. Hansel's back yard, and tossed it over the ledge. The creature instantly came to life and tried to escape, but it couldn't. As soon as we had tossed it over the ledge, it came alive . . . but it was also trapped. It couldn't fly back out. Finally, it flew off into the darkness below.

Back to Darkland.

"Let's go," I said. It was just past noon, and we still had a lot of places to look.

Ashley decided to go down Otsego street. I went along another side street, and it wasn't long before I found another gargoyle.

An old man and woman were standing in a driveway. They were staring at the statue right in front of their garage door, and they had confused looks on their faces.

But I think I knew what their problem was.

"What's the matter?" I said as I walked up their driveway. They both turned to look at me, and then turned their attention back to the strange stone gargoyle in their driveway.

"We have no idea how this got here," the old woman said. "When we woke up this morning, it was here."

"It's very strange," the old man said. "We didn't hear anything in the night. Someone must be playing a joke."

"Well, I think it's kind of cool," I said, standing next to them. "If you don't want it, I'll take it."

"We have no use for it," the woman said. "But tell me . . . how are you going to get it home?"

"I'll go get some help," I said. "Please? If you don't want it, I'd love to have it."

The old man nodded his head. "Well, we have to do something with it. We can't even get our car out of the garage until this thing gets moved."

"I'll be right back," I said, snapping my fingers as I turned. I ran a few blocks back to my house, but I didn't find Ashley or Mr. Hansel.

Now what? I thought. How would I get the gargoyle back to Mr. Hansel's?

Suddenly, I had an idea. My little brother has a red wagon! I could use the wagon to pull the gargoyle! I was sure it would work.

I pulled the wagon out of the garage and it rumbled behind me as I walked quickly back to the old man and woman's home. Their garage door was open, and the man was still in the driveway.

"Help me lift it," I asked as I pulled the wagon up alongside the gargoyle.

The man looked at me like he thought I was crazy! He laughed.

"Oh, there's no way that you and I alone can lift this," he said, smiling.

But I knew better.

"Well, let's just give it a try. If it doesn't work, then we'll try and figure out something else."

Boy, was he surprised when he found that we

could lift the statue without much problem at all! In a few seconds, the gargoyle was laying on its side in the wagon.

The man looked confused, and he scratched his head. "That sure is strange," he said.

"Well, I gotta go," I replied. "Thanks for the statue."

I was just about to pull the wagon away when he stopped me.

"Hold on a minute," he said. He was staring at the gargoyle, leaning closer to it. I didn't know what he was looking at.

"What's that?" he said, pointing.

I followed his finger to where he was looking.

Oh my gosh! The gargoyle's tongue! It was hanging out the side of its mouth, dangling like a dog's tongue on a hot summer day! *The old man had spotted the gargoyle's tongue!*

"What on earth is *that?*" The old man asked, peering even closer.

"Ah, um . . . it's . . . ."

What was I going to say?!?! I couldn't think of anything to tell him. If he realized that it was a real tongue, then he might find out!

Suddenly, I had an idea.

"Oh, it's only wet cement," I said as calmly as possible. "Someone must have just made this gargoyle last night. It looks like his tongue is about to fall off. I guess I'll have to fix it when I get home."

It worked! The old man seemed satisfied with the answer. "Oh, yes," he said. "That must be it. Well, thank you for getting rid of it for us. My wife, she didn't like the looks of this thing in our driveway. She gets the heebee-jeebees really easy, you know."

I waved good-bye as I pulled the wagon, not really sure what a 'heebee-jeebee' was, but glad that I'd found another gargoyle.

I searched and searched all day long. Actually, finding the gargoyles and taking them to Mr. Hansel's back yard wasn't as difficult as I thought. But it sure was tiring! I think I walked a hundred miles.

After I was sure I had searched every yard around for a dozen blocks, I stopped. I sat on Mr. Hansel's porch, waiting for Ashley and Mr. Hansel to return. I waited and waited, but they didn't show up.

Had something happened? Where could they be?

Finally, Mr. Hansel returned. He was carrying a big gargoyle in his arms, and he took it into his back yard and threw it over the ledge.

"Have you seen Ashley?" I asked him.

"No," he said, a look of concern on his face. "No, I haven't. Not since this afternoon."

Now I *was* worried. What if something had happened to Ashley? It was getting dark, and if we hadn't found all of the gargoyles, Ashley could be in trouble.

We *all* could be in trouble, for that matter.

It was getting dark fast, and there was still no sign of Ashley.

And then, my worst fears were confirmed. My worst fears were confirmed when I heard the loud flapping of wings. It had grown dark, and I looked up into the night sky.

Circling the air above me was a gargoyle—and it was carrying Ashley!

30

It was a horrible sight. The gargoyle held Ashley in its clutches as it swooped and dove through the air, swirling above Mr. Hansel's house.

"Come on!" Mr. Hansel shouted, and we darted through the gate into the back yard. The gargoyle continued to circle lower, and I almost couldn't bear to watch. I knew where he was going. I knew where he was taking Ashley.

Mr. Hansel and I stopped at the ledge. It was difficult to see, but the loud flapping of wings told us that the gargoyle—and Ashley—were close.

Suddenly the gargoyle was right in front of us! He was huge! He flapped his wings, and we could feel the whooshing of air as they swept up and down.

"Let me go!" I heard Ashley shout in the darkness. "Let me go right now!"

And then the gargoyle began speaking! He hovered in one place, just over the ledge, holding Ashley.

"You thought you could do it," the gargoyle hissed. *"You thought you could make us all return to Darkland forever, and you almost did. I am the last one left, but I will not go as easily as the others. Yes, I am returning to Darkland . . . but I am taking one of yours with me. This one will come with me, and remain in Darkland forever, and ever, and ever."*

"No!" I shouted. "You can't! Ashley is my friend!"

Ashley spoke up. I know she was terrified, but she was also mad! Ashley really can have a temper sometimes. "If you don't put me down, I'm going to bop you in the nose!" she screamed. "Put me down right now!"

The gargoyle ignored her.

"You see, you thought you could do it. You thought you could actually make us all return to Darkland. And yes, you have succeeded. But now, we

will have the last word. You have won, but it has cost you. It has cost you one of your own."

And with that, the gargoyle sank below the ledge, spinning into the darkness below. Ashley's horrified screams echoed through the darkness, and then faded away.

Ashley — my very best friend — was gone. She had been taken into Darkland by a gargoyle.

31

Mr. Hansel and I both must have had the same thought. We couldn't just stand by and let the gargoyle take Ashley. We both sprang for the door to the tunnel.

"Quickly!" Mr. Hansel said. "There is no time to lose!"

He didn't have to tell me twice!

Mr. Hansel unbolted the lock on the door and threw it open. I climbed down into the tunnel first.

"A flashlight!" he suddenly said. "We need a light."

I waited while he retrieved a flashlight from the house. He was only gone for a few seconds, but it seemed like hours.

He clicked the light on and slid down the ladder. For an old guy, he sure moved quick.

"Let's go!" he said, and we started our way down the winding tunnel. It was tough going at first, because the walls were so close. Mr. Hansel had a hard time because he had to walk sideways. I'm a lot smaller, so it was easier for me. Finally, the tunnel grew wide enough for us to run.

And that's what we did. We ran and ran, our footsteps echoing through the tunnel. Finally, we came to the door . . . the door to Darkland.

Mr. Hansel didn't waste any time. He opened the door slowly at first, to make sure there weren't any gargoyles hanging around. Then he opened it up all the way and stepped through. I followed.

Once again, we were in a strange world. I recognized the trees and the tall rock wall from the last time I was here. I didn't think I'd ever be back, but here I was. The sky was gray and dark, and everything looked spooky.

All of a sudden a movement caught my eye. Ashley!

She was on a ledge that stuck out from the

rock wall. She had spotted us, and she was waving frantically. I was relieved that she wasn't hurt . . . but now we had another problem: how was she going to get down? She was a long ways up, and there wasn't anyplace for her to go. She was stuck on the ledge, and below her was nothing but deep, dark water.

Boy, if I ever got my hands on that gargoyle, I'd strangle him!

Ashley looked like she was shouting something, but she was too far away. I couldn't hear a thing.

"She's going to have to jump," Mr. Hansel said, staring up at Ashley on the rock high above.

"Jump?!?!" I exclaimed. "But she'll be a goner for sure!"

"Well, both of you fell from the ledge that was even higher up than where she is," Mr. Hansel said.

"Yeah," I agreed. "But we also nearly got ate by a couple of gargoyles."

"Well, there's no other way," Mr. Hansel said. "She'll have to jump. She'll have to jump and swim to shore."

Mr. Hansel began waving his arm in the air, urging her to leap from the ledge. I did the same thing with my arm, but I wasn't sure if Ashley could see us very well. She was really a long ways away, high up into the sky on the ledge.

Suddenly a movement caught my attention, and when I realized what it was, my whole body froze in shock.

Because I knew what it was.

I knew what it was, and I knew that Ashley was a goner.

32

I had never seen a bigger, meaner, nastier, uglier-looking gargoyle than what I saw right then. It swooped through the sky like a plane. It was so BIG! It had long teeth and a huge tongue that slashed from side to side. It was a dark red color, except for his eyes. His eyes were the darkest black I had ever seen.

Mr. Hansel stopped waving. He looked just as afraid as I was!

"Quick! Duck down!" Mr. Hansel hissed. He dove toward a rock ledge and I was right on his

heels. I didn't want that huge thing to see me!

A shadow fell over us. It was the gargoyle. I sure hoped he couldn't see us! And I hoped he couldn't see Ashley, either.

But it was too late.

The gargoyle drifted over us, swooped back up over the water.

And saw Ashley.

The giant creature seemed to hang in the air, just looking at her. Ashley was standing on the ledge, with nowhere to go.

She was helpless. There was nothing she could do.

The gargoyle flew closer to Ashley. Ashley backed up against the ledge as far as she could, but there was nowhere for her to go, no route of escape.

The gargoyle flew closer still, watching her, its tongue lashing from side to side. It looked like it was getting ready to attack.

I couldn't take it any longer. I didn't know if Ashley would be able to hear me or see me, but I just couldn't stand there and do nothing.

Suddenly, I burst out from under the rock ledge.

"ASHLEY!" I cried at the very top of my lungs. *"JUMP! JUMP INTO THE WATER!"*

Just then, the gargoyle turned its head.

It had spotted me! It had spotted me, but what happened next was exactly what I had hoped. The gargoyle was looking down at me . . . and that gave Ashley her chance! She leapt forward, leaping into the air, and began falling feet-first to the water below! The gargoyle had been paying attention to me, and hadn't even seen Ashley until she splashed into the water!

The terrible creature spun around and swooped down, letting out a screech that I'll never forget. It was a screech of anger and madness, and I knew that we had really made him furious.

But the worst was yet to come.

Ashley's head popped up from beneath the surface. She sputtered and gasped and coughed.

"Look out Ashley!" I shouted, as the gargoyle swooped down to grab her. Ashley ducked beneath the surface just in time, and the gargoyle's claws scraped the top of the water.

He had missed!

Ashley's head popped up again, and again the gargoyle attacked. Again, Ashley was able to catch a quick breath and pop below the surface. Again, the gargoyle missed, and he was becoming angrier and angrier.

"We have to help her!" Mr. Hansel cried. Ashley was having a hard time trying to duck from the gargoyle. Every time the creature attacked, she was forced to go back under water. It wouldn't be long before she became exhausted.

"But what can we do?" I asked.

As soon as I asked the question, I got my answer . . . because the gargoyle had grown tired of trying to capture Ashley — and now he was about to attack *me!*

33

Without any warning, the huge gargoyle came swooping toward us . . . wings flapping, mouth snapping open and closed, tongue lashing from side to side. Its black eyes burned with fury.

And it was coming right for me! There was nothing I could do.

Suddenly, Mr. Hansel was by my side. He was carrying an enormous stick! Actually, it was more like a log. It was long and heavy, and he swung it in the air like a baseball bat. I ducked down and let the big stick swing past.

And it worked! It slowed the gargoyle's attack, and Mr. Hansel brought the stick up again, this time poking it toward the gargoyle. The creature darted from side to side, trying to get around, but Mr. Hansel was too quick.

"Hurry!" he shouted. "Run over to the door! Run over to the door and I'll try and hold him off!"

"Corky!" a voice suddenly shouted,

Ashley! She had made it to shore! She had made it to shore, and now she was emerging from the water, soaking wet.

I began to run, and pointed toward the door in the rock wall.

"Over there!" I shouted to her. "To the door!"

I didn't have to tell her again! She suddenly sprang from the shore, sprinting toward the rock wall. I was doing the same, and when I turned, I caught a glimpse of Mr. Hansel. He was still hard at work, fending off the attacking gargoyle. I hoped he would be all right.

Ashley reached the door first and she threw it open and bolted inside. I quickly followed, throwing the door almost completely closed behind me. Both Ashley and I were out of breath, and we peered out the crack of the door, watching the strange event near the water. Mr. Hansel was busy

154

keeping the gargoyle at bay, lunging toward the creature with the big stick. The gargoyle was flying a few feet from the ground, swinging from side to side to get out of the way of the stick.

"Mr. Hansel!" I shouted. "Come on! We made it! Run!"

Mr. Hansel snapped his head around just long enough to see that we were safely behind the door. Suddenly, he dropped the stick and began to run! He sprang toward us, and we opened the door farther so that he could run right into the tunnel.

That was, *if* he made it! The gargoyle was close behind, wings flapping madly. It was hissing and screeching, and it seemed angrier than ever.

"Come on, Mr. Hansel!" Ashley shouted. "Come on!"

Closer . . . .

"You're almost here!" I shouted. "Faster!"

I threw the door open and Mr. Hansel bounded inside. The gargoyle was right behind him, but Ashley and I grabbed the old wood door and pulled as hard as we could. The door slammed shut just an instant before the gargoyle would have reached us.

Mr. Hansel was panting and out of breath. He reached out and pulled the bolt across the door and locked it.

Just beyond the door, in Darkland, we could hear the gargoyle screeching in anger. It flew around and near the door for a few minutes, until finally there were no more sounds. The gargoyle had left.

We walked in silence back up through the strange rock tunnel. Not one of us said a word. The only sounds were our feet echoing off the stone wall.

Finally, we were at the ladder. Ashley was first, then me, then Mr. Hansel. Once again we were in Mr. Hansel's backyard, standing in the gloomy darkness.

"That was close," Ashley said quietly.

"Too close," I said, nodding my head. "Way too close."

Mr. Hansel closed the door, and locked it.

"Yes, but now, we'll never have to worry about gargoyles ever again," he said.

I wasn't sure what he meant.

"What do you mean?" I asked. "Can't the gargoyles escape? Won't they still be able to get out?"

Mr. Hansel shook his head. "My job is finished here, and yours is too. It is time for me to return."

Huh? Return where?

"You see," he continued, "as the Gatewatcher, it is my responsibility to bring all of the gargoyles back to Darkland. Only when all of the gargoyles have returned, can I go back home myself."

"Home?" Ashley asked. "But . . . you are home." She waved her arm around, indicating where he was. "This is *your* house."

Mr. Hansel shook his head. "Yes, and no," he said. "I have lived here on earth in this home, simply to finish my job. Now that my job is done, I can return."

I was puzzled. "Return? Return to where?"

"Why, to Darkland, of course." And with that, he took a step back. "Allow me," he began, "to show you something. Do not be afraid."

I know this will be hard to believe, but what was about to happen was even stranger and more terrifying than anything I had seen so far . . . .

157

34

. . . . because Mr. Hansel began to change! His body began twisting and turning. His arms grew thicker, and so did his legs. Wings began to sprout out of his back! His face grew wide, and his nose turned up. It didn't take a rocket scientist to figure out that Mr. Hansel was changing . . . *into a gargoyle!*

It was crazy! Ashley and I both took a step back, and then another. Then another.

We stopped. So did Mr. Hansel. I don't know how long we stood there, looking at each other. I could feel my heart thumping in my chest.

I held my breath.

"Now you know," Mr. Hansel said. "I am a gargoyle. I know I told you that I wasn't, but at the time, it would have frightened you too much. Now that all of the gargoyles have returned to Darkland, I can go there myself. It is time for me to go home."

This was all too crazy to believe . . . and yet, somehow, it made sense.

"But I thought all gargoyles turned to stone during the day," I said.

Mr. Hansel nodded his gargoyle head. "Yes, you are right," he said. "But the Gatewatcher can take the form of a human. When I do, I am no longer bound by the laws of gargoyles."

I had a lot of questions that I wanted to ask, but it didn't look like I would get them answered—because Mr. Hansel suddenly began to flap his wings! He took to the air and hovered above us.

"It is time for me to return," he said. "I must say good-bye."

"Wait!" I shouted. "Wait! I want to ask you—"

But it was too late. Mr. Hansel was already flying off. He took one last look at us before slipping over the ledge . . . into Darkland.

Ashley and I ran to the edge of the canyon in

the backyard, just in time to see the big, gargoyle-shape of Mr. Hansel disappear into the darkness below.

"Like . . . did this just happen?" Ashley asked.

"I think it did," I said, still staring into the dark depths. "But this is just too weird. Imagine! Mr. Hansel was a gargoyle all along!"

We stood at the edge for a few more moments, just gazing down into the darkness.

"Come on," I said finally. "Let's go."

We walked through the dark yard and opened the gate. Sure enough, as soon as we stepped out of the back yard, the late evening sun was shining down.

Crazy. Totally crazy.

"I gotta go home before I miss dinner," Ashley said.

"Yeah, me too," I replied. "Are you going to tell anyone about this?"

She shook her head. "No way," she answered. "No one would believe me, anyway. They'd think I was nuts."

"Me too," I said. "But, I'm glad it worked out. I'm glad Mr. Hansel was able to go home."

"Yeah," Ashley said. "See you tomorrow?"

"Yep," I said. "Watch out for gargoyles tonight." I laughed, and so did Ashley. She turned and walked across Mr. Hansel's front lawn, then across her own lawn, to her house. I turned and began walking home.

The sun was still up, but it had fallen beneath the trees, and it was growing dark quickly.

Still, when something caught my eye in my front yard, I could see what it was.

I froze.

It can't be, I thought. *It just can't be.*

It was.

On the grass in our front yard was a great big, ugly, gargoyle!

35

I stopped. I stared. I couldn't move. A lump formed in my throat.

This can't be, I thought. *All of the gargoyles have returned to Darkland. That's why Mr. Hansel was able to go home.*

I skirted my yard, keeping my eye on the gargoyle. Creeping along in front of the house, I tiptoed over the porch and slipped inside.

Mom was watching TV. "There you are," she said.

I had to tell her. I had to tell her what was in

the yard.

"Mom," I began, "have you seen what's in our front yard?"

Mom looked puzzled for a moment. "Oh, *that*," she said, laughing. "Your father bought it at a garage sale today. Isn't it the ugliest thing you've ever seen?"

I nodded. "Yeah," I said. "It's gross."

"He's not leaving it there. I think he's going to put it out back in the garden tomorrow morning."

I told Mom that I was tired and that I was going to bed. But there was one thing that I needed to do first.

I took the flashlight from the kitchen drawer and slipped back outside.

I had to know. I had to know for sure that the gargoyle wasn't real.

I clicked on the flashlight and walked across the lawn, approaching the gargoyle from behind. It was completely dark by now, and crickets whirred in the cool night air. I tip-toed slowly through the damp grass.

Slowly . . . .

Almost there . . . .

I shined the light on the huge beast as I walked around to face it. It sure was ugly.

I drew a deep breath, leaned closer, and

shined the flashlight into the mouth of the gargoyle. The tongue was made of . . . .

36

Cement!

Whew! It was only a statue, after all! A wave of relief rolled through my body, and I smiled.

Thank goodness, I thought, clicking off the flashlight and walking back to the house. *Thank goodness.*

When I woke up the next morning, I bounded right up out of bed and went to my window. I guess I expected to see another gargoyle in the yard, but I didn't.

Later that day, I met Ashley in the park, and we talked about our mysterious adventure. We both agreed that it was probably the strangest thing that has ever happened to either of us.

But another strange thing was about to happen.

When we walked home, there was a large moving van parked in front of Mr. Hansel's house! There were people unloading things and carrying them into the house. What in the world was going on?!?!?

Then I spotted them: three kids, about our age. One girl and two boys. Actually, one of the boys was a lot younger than us. They were running through the yard. Suddenly, they all disappeared — into Mr. Hansel's back yard!

"Oh no!" I said to Ashley. "We've got to go warn them!"

We ran across the street and bolted through the yard. Someone said 'hello' to me but I didn't stop to answer. We had to get to Mr. Hansel's back yard before it was too late.

But when I reached the fence and ran through the gate, nothing happened.

There was nothing there!

I stopped. So did Ashley.

We were looking at a normal, everyday back

yard in the city of Gaylord. There was grass and a couple trees, and a birdbath. It wasn't dark like it had been yesterday.

And there was no sign of Darkland. There was no ledge that dropped off into darkness, no door that went to a secret tunnel. It looked just like our back yard looked.

"Hi!" I heard someone shout. I turned. A girl was walking toward us.

"Hello," I said. "Are you—"

"Moving in?" she finished. "Yep." She smiled "We just got here."

"I'm Corky," I said, "and this is my friend Ashley."

"Hi," she said. "I'm Erin Barnes. Those are my brothers, over there." She pointed to the two boys running through the yard. The oldest one spotted us, and came over.

"Hi," he said, and we introduced ourselves to him. His name was Kevin; his younger brother was Bobby.

"You're . . . you're moving in?" I asked. "Today?"

"Sure," Kevin said. Erin nodded her head.

I guess I was just waiting for something to happen, for a gargoyle to come swooping out of the sky and snatch one of us away.

But nothing happened.

"My dad knows the guy who used to live here," Kevin said. "That's who we bought it from."

Even more strange. I didn't think anybody knew Mr. Hansel. .

As it turned out, we were all to become good friends. Erin was a couple years older than me. Kevin was twelve, and we got along great. Bobby was only six, and he spent most of his time playing in the yard, doing things that all six-year-olds do.

One day I almost told Kevin about the gargoyles. Kevin had spotted the gargoyle in our garden — the one dad bought at a garage sale.

"That's kinda cool," he said.

"Maybe one day I'll tell you my gargoyle story," I said. "It's really strange. It's strange, weird, and spooky, all rolled into one."

"I've got a story like that," Kevin said. "And it happened just a few weeks before we moved here."

"Really?" I said. "Like what?"

"Well, my family went camping in St. Ignace. It's a city on the other side of the Mackinac Bridge."

I knew where the Mackinac Bridge was. It was the bridge that connected Michigan's upper and lower peninsulas together.

"What happened?" I asked.

"Well, first of all, Erin and Bobby and I got lost in the woods. And I mean *lost*. Totally."

"How did you find your way back?" I asked. I really wanted to know, just in case I ever got lost in the woods.

Kevin looked around to make sure no one else was listening.

"Well, I know this is going to be hard to believe, but we were helped by an Indian spirit," he said. "Wanna hear about it?"

"Are you kidding?" I replied. "Start from the beginning!"

And so he did.

**Next in the 'Michigan Chillers'
series . . . .
#6 : 'Strange Spirits of St. Ignace'
Go to the next page for a few
chilling chapters!**

"Well, that looks like it's the last of it. Are you all packed, Kevin?"

Dad stood next to our car, hands on his hips, gazing into the open trunk. He looked up at the duffle bags strapped on the roof.

"You bet," I answered. "Let's go. I've been waiting for this all summer!"

The morning sky was blue and clear. A perfect day to begin our vacation. I could see some of my friends in their yards, looking wishfully toward us. They all knew what we were doing; they all wished that they could go. Even David Skinner, my best friend, said that he would give me his new football if he could go. I asked Dad, but he said no. He liked David, but he said that this was a family trip. Maybe some other time.

Dad closed the trunk, and hopped into the car.

We were on our way.

Camping. Not only camping, but camping up north. St. Ignace, Michigan, to be exact. St. Ignace is the first city you come to on the other side of the Mackinac Bridge. It's one of the oldest cities in Michigan. One of the first people to live there was Father Jaques Marquette. He lived there from 1666 till the time he died in 1675.

But even before that, there were other people there.

Indians.

The forest was very special to them, and there is a lot of Indian history all around St. Ignace. Camping there sure was going to be a lot of fun.

I've never been camping before. Neither has my sister, Erin, or Bobby, my younger brother.

Well, okay — we've camped in our back yard a few times. It's kind of fun. We pitch a tent and roast marshmallows, and Dad tells scary stories. Once he told us a story that was so scary, Bobby started to cry! He wouldn't spend the night in the tent with us, and wound up staying in his bed in the house that night. What a baby.

But this camping trip would be different. We would be camping in the forest—in the wild, with trees and birds and animals. I hear that there are bears in northern Michigan. I hoped I would see one!

What I didn't know was that we would see a bear all right . . . and a lot of other things that I wouldn't have believed myself . . . except the things happened to *me,* so I know it was real. Let me just say this: If you're going to spend any time in the forest, you'd better know what you're doing.

But I was prepared. I had a brand new pocketknife, and an outdoor survival handbook. Which, at the moment, was in the hands of my sister.

"Can I *please* have my book back," I pleaded. She'd been reading it since breakfast. I thought I was being nice by letting her borrow it, but she'd had it for an hour.

"Fine," she said, slapping the book closed and tossing it into my lap. She shook her head and rolled her eyes.

That's just like my sister. We get along well enough, but she can be pretty snappy sometimes.

She's 13 . . . a year older than I am . . . so she thinks that she's the boss.

Right.

"Can I see it?" Bobby asked from his seat in the car.

"Yeah, when I'm through," I said. "I just got it and I haven't even been able to read it myself yet." I shot a glare at Erin, who ignored me like she usually does.

I opened the book in my lap. It's very cool. There are different sections that tell you what kinds of trees and plants and animals you'll find in the woods. It has a section on how to survive on edible plants, and how to cook them. And it shows you which plants to stay away from. There are a lot of plants in the woods that, if eaten, are deadly poisonous. You really have to know what you're doing if you're going to eat wild plants and berries and things. You just can't wander into the woods and start eating the first green leaf you find!

There is a lot more in the book as well. It shows you how to start a fire without any matches, how to build a lean-to, how to catch fish . . . all kinds of things. When we got to our camp site, I was going to see if I could do some of the things that were in the book.

I shoved my hand in my pocket and pulled

out my knife. I had saved for it and bought it at the sporting goods store. It was a good knife, too. The handle was made of wood and had a deer carved into it. It had four different folding blades, each one a different length. The knife had taken every penny that I'd saved, but I thought it was worth it.

Of course, at the time, I didn't know just how valuable that knife was going to be . . . because soon, that pocket knife was going to save our lives.

The drive to St. Ignace took us about six hours. Six *boring* hours, I might add. Bobby fell asleep the minute we left the driveway, and he slept most of the way. Dad and Mom and Erin and I played games. We made up a different name for different kinds of cars, and then when we saw one, we would call out its name. The object, of course, was to be the first to spot a car. You got a point for each one you saw, and I was doing great. I usually win at this game.

At about the half-way point, Erin and I got

into a huge fight. She saw a giant semi-truck carrying six vans . . . and she counted them all as points. I was sure it had to be illegal . . . but we didn't have a rule book, so Dad said that she could count the points.

That put her four points ahead of me, and we fought about it all the way till we reached the Mackinac Bridge. Dad got so mad at Erin and I that he threatened to turn the car around and go home.

Bobby woke up just as we started across the Mackinac Bridge. Let me tell you, if you've never crossed it before, it's really something to see. It's five miles long, and hundreds of feet in the air. Boats in the water below look like tiny bugs. We even saw a big freighter passing right below us. It was cool.

But it was the other side of Mackinac Bridge that I was excited about. Because right on the other side of the bridge was St. Ignace.

We were going camping.

As we made our way across the bridge, I shoved my hand into my pocket again just to make sure my knife was still there. Then I fumbled through my outdoor survival book again, looking at the pictures and drawings. I couldn't wait.

We wouldn't be camping at a campground, either. Dad knows a man who has a lot of property not far from town. Dad says that it's nothing but forest and swamp land for miles and miles. No homes, no roads, no people — just forest. Trees and swamps. And animals and bugs and birds.

It was time for dinner, so we ate at a restaurant in St. Ignace. From where I sat, I could see ferry boats taking people across Lake Michigan to Mackinac Island. Summertime sure is a busy place in St. Ignace.

After dinner, we got back in the car and started to drive. Soon, Dad turned off the highway onto a small dirt road. After a few bumpy miles, the dirt road turned into a beaten two-track. It was obvious that there hadn't been anyone back here in a long, long time.

Erin had fallen asleep, and I couldn't resist giving her a bumblebee. That's when you stick your finger right near someone's ear when they're sleeping. As you just barely touch their ear, you make a buzzing sound. Because they're sleeping, the person thinks that there's a bee in their ear.

"*Bzzzzzzz . . . .*"

Well, Erin freaked out. *Totally*. It was great! She snapped awake and slapped the side of her head to smack the 'bee' that had been 'buzzing' by her ear. It was all I could do to keep myself from laughing. When she saw the silly grin on my face, she was *hot*.

"Knock it off, Kevin!" she screamed at me. "Mom! Dad! Tell Kevin to knock it off!"

I quickly flipped open my outdoor survival handbook and pretended that I had been reading.

"What?" I said innocently, looking up from the book. "I've been reading. What's your problem?"

"You're going to get it," she hissed, slugging me in the shoulder. Bobby started giggling. "You too," Erin said, turning to glare at him. *"You're* going to get it if you don't wipe that little smirk off your face."

The car came to a sudden stop, and Mom and Dad opened the doors. I hopped out and looked around.

Trees. All around us was nothing but trees. The two-track road that we'd been traveling on was hardly even noticeable. It was all gown over with long green grass and small shrubs.

The sounds of the forest filled the air. There were birds and crickets, and a light *shussshhh* of wind as it crept through the trees. There were no car horns, no airplanes. No tires on pavement, no yelling on the street corner. All we could hear were the sounds of the forest.

"Okay gang," Dad began as he began

lowering duffle bags from the roof of the car. "Let's get these bags unpacked."

It was total confusion for a little while. I think Dad wanted us to believe that he's a good camper, but he sure wasn't having much luck with one of the tents. The poles kept coming apart and the tent would fall down. Dad was frustrated and saying things under his breath. Mom stood by trying to help, but Dad said that he'd done this a thousand times and he could do it himself.

As for my tent, it was already up. I have a small two-person tent that I practiced setting up in the back yard of our house. That's where Erin and I would sleep. Mom, Dad, and Bobby would sleep in the bigger tent right next to ours.

That is, if Dad was able to keep it from collapsing.

Finally, just before it got dark, he got the tent up. We left a lot of gear in the car, because Dad said that we would be hiking back to another camping spot in the morning. We could leave the gear in the car for tonight, then load it into our packs in the morning.

As I lay awake in the dark tent, I thought about our trip. It was a dream come true. Here we were, camping in the wilds of northern Michigan. I had a new knife, and a new outdoor survival handbook.

This was going to be cool. The adventure of a lifetime. After a while, I fell asleep to the sounds of a million crickets.

How long I slept, I don't know . . . but I awoke to the sound of screaming! A shrill painful wailing pierced the darkness. It didn't take me long to figure out who it was.

Dad!

Dad was screaming at the top of his lungs! Then Mom started screaming, too! When grownups scream like that, you can be sure that whatever is happening can't be good!

3

I snapped up in my sleeping bag, and so did Erin. What was it?!?! What was wrong?!?!

A light clicked on in the tent next to us. Dad and Mom were still screaming their heads off.

Oh no! I thought. *What's happened to Mom and Dad?!?! What if something happened to Bobby?!?!?*

Now I could hear frantic shuffling, and in the darkness I fumbled for my pocketknife. I had set it on the floor of the tent next to my pillow. I found it instantly, and gripped it tightly. I unzipped the tent flap.

"What are you doing?!?!" Erin stammered.

"I want to know what's going on!" I said. "Mom and Dad are in trouble!" In the next instant I had slipped out of my sleeping bag and outside.

The ground was cold and clammy on my feet. I stood in front of my tent, gripping my still-folded knife, but ready to use it if I had to.

Mom and Dad were out of the tent, and they were shining their flashlight beams at one another. They looked silly like that, Dad in his pajamas and mom in a nightgown. They were hopping up and down and brushing themselves off.

"Ouch!" Dad yelped, as he swept his had over his chest. "There's another one!" Mom was doing the same thing.

"What's wrong?" I asked, running up to them.

"Ants!" Dad answered, smacking his hand on his arm. "Ouch! We set up the tent on an ant's nest!"

There's a time in your life when you just want to roll over on the ground laughing. Sometimes it's just better to hold it in and not let anyone know that you're laughing inside.

This was one of those times. But I'll never forget the site of Mom and Dad, in the glow of the flashlight beams, hoping up and down, brushing ants off each other.

Somehow, Bobby slept right through the whole ordeal. The ants hadn't bothered him (I would tease him later about not being tasty enough). Regardless, Mom and Dad had to wake him up so that they could move the tent to another place. A place without ants.

Finally, after about an hour of stumbling and fumbling in the dark, Mom and Dad had moved the tent and went back to sleep.

But I was wide awake.

I found my small pen light and clicked it on beneath my sleeping bag, and opened my outdoor survival handbook. It was so cool. There was so much to learn about the outdoors, so much to make and do. I really hoped that I would have a chance to make some of the things in the book. Maybe I could even find the right kind of plants and berries to eat. The book said that this was the season for blueberries, so I was going to be on the lookout for those.

After a while, I grew tired and was able to fall asleep.

When I awoke in the morning, I was the first up. I climbed out of the tent and stood. It was real early, and the sky was a rich, bright pink. Birds were singing, and the air was fresh and sweet. The sun would be up in a few minutes.

I was about to gather up some dead branches for the morning fire, but when I looked at the ground, I stopped.

There were strange tracks on the ground. Not just tracks, but *animal* tracks. *Huge* ones.

I kneeled down to the ground. The tracks were big . . . bigger than my hand. And they were definitely animal tracks. I stood up and followed them around our campsite. Whatever it was, it had been all over our campsite during the night!

I followed the tracks around and around . . . and they led right to the door of Mom and Dad's tent!

"Mom?" I whispered hoarsely. "Dad? Are you guys all right?"

I heard shuffling inside the tent.

"Yeah, fine," I heard Dad say groggily. "Why?"

"There are tracks all over the place out here," I said, looking down at the prints in the ground.

"Probably a raccoon," Dad said from inside the tent. I heard more shuffling, and he unzipped the tent flap and stepped out into the cool morning air. Dad's got these silly striped pajamas that look

189

ridiculous. But I wouldn't tell him that!

He looked at the tracks on the ground. "No, these definitely aren't raccoon tracks. I think these are bear tracks."

Holy cow! A bear had been walking right through our camp site! Cool! I wish I had been awake to see it!

Erin was awake now, and she came out of the tent. Mom and Bobby were stirring as well. They all came out to see the big tracks that criss-crossed our camp site.

"He was looking for food," Dad said. "It's a good thing we left the food in the car. He would have torn everything to shreds to get at it."

"But what will we do when we can't keep the food in the car?" Erin asked.

Good question.

"We'll throw a rope over a tree branch, tie all of our food up, and pull it up into the air. That way, the bear can't reach it."

I'd heard of that trick before. It made sense. At least, more sense than setting your tent up on an ant's nest.

But there was something strange about these bear tracks. I couldn't put my finger on it right away, but I knew there was something odd about them.

I was in charge of making the morning fire, and, after breakfast, we packed everything up and broke camp. All of us had backpacks. Even Bobby. He couldn't carry much, but he had a little pack and was excited about carrying it. Dad locked up the car, made a check of the site, and we started to walk along the old two-track.

We were on our way.

We walked for what seemed like hours. Erin got tired and started to whine about it. I was tired, too, but I kept my mouth shut. I was surprised at Bobby. For as young as he was, he held out great. He walked right along behind me, whistling and humming most of the day. He only complained a couple of times.

Finally, when we reached a small stream, Dad decided that it was time to stop for the night.

We set up camp, and Dad was careful to make sure that there were no ants around. I don't think he wanted to go through what he did the night before.

After the tents were up, Dad built a fire and we roasted hot dogs. They were great. Mom promised us that, after it got dark, we could roast marshmallows before we went to bed.

Erin and Bobby and I had the task of washing

the dinner plates. Really, there wasn't much to wash, because we had cooked the hot dogs on sticks. All we had to wash were some cups and a few plates. But I hate washing the dishes, anyway.

We took the dishes to the stream, and it was there that I noticed the tracks — *the same tracks we'd seen this morning at the other camp site!*

"Erin, look," I said, pointing to the mud near the stream. "Look . . . those are the same tracks we saw this morning."

Erin bent down and peered at the tracks. "I just hope he stays away from us," she said.

"Wanna go find him?" I asked.

"What?!?! You want to go find a bear?!?!"

"Come on," I urged. "It'll be fun. We'll stay away from him. A long ways. I promise."

Erin bit her lower lip, thinking for a moment. "Well, only if we don't go far," she said finally. "I don't think Mom and Dad would want us going very far from camp."

I went back to my tent and grabbed my outdoor survival handbook and walked back to where the stream was. I opened the handbook to the section on animal tracks.

"Look at this," I said to Erin. "Take a look at these tracks." Erin looked at the drawings of tracks in the handbook. "Now look at *these* tracks," I said, pointing to the mud.

"Yeah? So?" she began. "They're bear tracks, just like Dad said."

"But look closer, Erin," I said. "Look at the tracks in the mud. *They have six claws. The tracks in the mud have six claws . . . the ones in my handbook only have five.*"

Erin shuddered. "That's weird," she said. "I'm not sure I want to go looking for a six-clawed bear."

"Oh, come on," I said.

Suddenly, another voice spoke up. "Where we goin' you guys?"

Bobby.

"We're going for a walk to look for the terrible six-clawed bear," I said. As I spoke, I raised my hands and made claws. Bobby's eyes got huge. "I wanna go," he said excitedly.

"All right," I answered. "But you have to be quiet. Six-clawed bears don't like noises. Especially noises made by little Bobbies."

And with that, we were off. The sun was still above the trees, and there was still a few good hours of light left. We followed the strange six-clawed tracks as they wound along the stream. Then, they took a turn and went though a swamp. Soon, we came to the edge of a dark forest. The trees grew tall and thick. The tracks led into the forest.

"I think we should go back," Erin said. "It'll be dark soon. Mom and Dad aren't going to want us out after dark."

"Yeah, you're right," I said. "Let's head back."

I was about to turn and begin walking back when Bobby's hand suddenly shot out.

"Look!" he squealed.

I looked in the direction that he was pointing, and all of a sudden, I saw it.

Not forty feet away.

A bear.

He was standing near a tree . . . and he was looking right at us!

I froze.

Erin froze.

Bobby froze.

In the growing darkness, we could see the huge shape of the bear. I could see his ears, his nose, and his open mouth.

And I could see his teeth. They were absolutely huge . . . the biggest, nastiest teeth I had ever seen. It was incredible!

But what happened next I couldn't believe. *Right before our eyes the bear vanished! He disappeared while we were watching him!* He turned this strange misty white, and then . . . he was gone. It was like he evaporated into thin air.

Just like that.

"D-d-d . . . did . . . y-y-you just s-s-see that?" Erin stammered.

"Holy cow," I whispered. *"That bear just disappeared right before our eyes!"*

"Neat-o!" Bobby said. "I got to see a bear disappear!" Bobby was too young to realize that what we had just witnessed was really crazy. Bobby probably thought all bears could just vanish like that.

"Let's go," Erin said. "I don't like this. I don't like this at all."

I wasn't going to argue. I turned and looked at the ground to follow our tracks through the swamp. The sun was now almost completely beneath the trees, and it had grown darker just within the past few minutes.

But when I looked to find our tracks, they were *gone!* When we walked through the swamp the first time, our feet left big imprints in the soft earth. Now they had *vanished!* Our tracks had vanished—just like the strange bear.

We trudged through the swamp, searching for our footprints.

"They have to be around here somewhere," I said.

But the farther we walked, the more I began to realize that we might have a problem. The woods had grown dark, and all I had was a small pen light. I clicked it on and swept the ground. I still couldn't find our tracks.

Erin said it first. I hadn't wanted to hear the words, even though I had thought them.

"Kevin . . . are we . . . are we . . . *lost?*" she asked.

That's what I didn't want to hear.

Lost.

Hearing this, Bobby began to cry. "Are we lost?" he sniffled.

"No, we're fine," I assured him. "We're not lost. We'll be back at the camp in no time."

But the fact was, I knew better.

We *were* lost. We were lost in a forest.

"Okay, let's stay calm," Erin said, but her words weren't very convincing. Her voice trembled as she spoke, and I knew she was frightened.

"What we need to do is —" I stopped in mid-sentence.

Crunch.

I heard a noise in the woods. We were in complete darkness now, and a half moon was

197

beginning to creep up over the trees. Stars blanketed the sky.

Crunch. It was closer.

Erin and Bobby and I huddled together.

Crunch. Cru-crunch. Crunch. The crunching was loud, like something heavy was making them.

Like a bear.

The closer the noise came, the tighter Bobby and Erin and I huddled together. Whatever it was, it was only a few feet from us.

I held my breath. What could it be? There was something coming toward us, crunching through the underbrush.

What if it *was* the bear? What if he was looking for food? What if . . . *we were his supper?!?!*

"What is it?" Erin's whisper trembled in my ear.

"I don't know," I answered, *"but I'm going to find out."* Bravely, I reached into my pocket and pulled out my pocketknife, along with my pen light.

"What are you going to do?" she whispered.

"You'll see," I said.

And with that, I opened up my knife, ready for action. I drew a deep breath, held out my pen light, aimed it in the direction of the noise—and turned it on . . . .

GARGOYLES OF GAYLORD CROSSWORD PUZZLE!

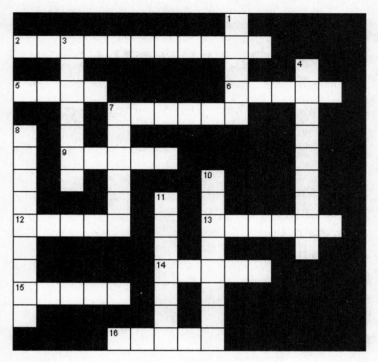

ACROSS

2. Another word for 'vanished' (PG. 126)
5. Mr Hansel's _____ (PG. 39)
6. A_____ tower (PG 61)
7. Frightened (PG. 117)
9. Large birds (PG. 93)
12. _____ being (PG. 97)
13. _____ with wings (PG. 60)
14. Ashley falls from a _____ (PG. 81)
15. Type of claw (PG. 64)
16. Used to fly (PG. 159)

DOWN

1. _____ old man (PG. 125)
3. Odd (PG. 168)
4. A bad dream (PG. 40)
7. Corky's younger brother (PG. 29)
8. Very large animals (PG 100)
10. How many stars? (PG. 44)
11. _____ drawer (PG. 164)

WORD PUZZLE!

Unscramble the letters to form the correct word

1. FSTEEANLP   _ _ _ _ _ _ _ _ _

2. CSMSBKOA   KECER   _ _ _ _ _ _ _ _   _ _ _ _ _

3. GEYSLOARG   _ _ _ _ _ _ _ _ _

4. ANGHIMCI   _ _ _ _ _ _ _ _

5. KOYRC   _ _ _ _ _

6. YRAGDLO   _ _ _ _ _ _ _

7. SEUTTA   _ _ _ _ _ _

8. HYALSE   _ _ _ _ _ _

9. EOGSOT ERSETT   _ _ _ _ _ _   _ _ _ _ _ _

10. LSCWA   _ _ _ _ _

GARGOYLES OF GAYLORD WORD SEARCH!

```
J W P G U O E H D V S E X R A X V L W U
T V O G M Z N N J A C Y N X W K Y E Q W
Y N V T O O A G O I L N H F I E G E D D
M C Q Z S L C K A T X W Z E R A A R Y K
B Q S F K E W L V H S O Z H T Z Y A X C
R M P R M G G V A I G Q R E R K L P H H
B V A E E A G O E W A Y W H R X O A U N
Y D N R Y L M I S N S A G O L C R K A J
S T J R G L L I R T T D C X R M D E N W
X D M W W I R I T C R K O D J L C E H B
T I C B X V J S H B N E C X S D I R K Z
A I T O Y E X E G C T X E D K Y J C O N
U R S W G N R G I S N C N T S A L K U A
W J M E Z I E E L S S A E A R F D C B W
B G B R F P C U H G R L G Y C X X A C Q
E J A S H L E Y S N U P M I B Q J B Z O
T J K J E A F I A I Z E T B H X G S R D
K A F V X U N H L W D N U B Z C S S Z C
A U F E F O T S F K D F Y P X O I O V F
D S E H N A S A E C F E T F T R V M B J
E H Q U N E W H T L N S E L Y O G R A G
G E Z H U C Z F Y S G T L M M E U T U J
T L O O P D Q X V Z N J E W G R P C H V
U J U J Q A E U R H N Z E H P X R E G A
```

Gaylord
Gargoyles
Mr. Hansel
Corky
Ashley
Otsego Street
Alpine Village
Alpenfest
Mossback Creek
Stone

Cement
Claws
Wings
Darkland
Gatewatcher
Flashlight
Statues
Michigan Chillers
Johnathan Rand

About the author

Johnathan Rand is the author of the best-selling **'Chillers'** series, now with over 1,000,000 copies in print. In addition to the **'Chillers'** series, Rand is also the author of **'Ghost in the Graveyard',** a collection of thrilling, original short stories featuring *The Adventure Club*. (And don't forget to check out **www.ghostinthegraveyard.com** and read an **entire story** from 'Ghost in the Graveyard' *FREE!*) When Mr. Rand and his wife are not traveling to schools and book signings, they live in a small town in northern lower Michigan with their two dogs, Abby and Salty. He still writes all of his books in the wee hours of the morning, and still submits all manuscripts by mail. He is currently working on his newest series, entitled **'American Chillers'**. His popular website features hundreds of photographs, stories, and art work. Visit:

WWW.AMERICANCHILLERS.COM

Also by Johnathan Rand:

GHOST IN THE GRAVEYARD

NOW AVAILABLE! OFFICIAL 'MICHIGAN & AMERICAN CHILLERS' WEARABLES, INCLUDING:

-EMBROIDERED HATS
-EMBROIDERED T-SHIRTS
-BACKPACKS

VISIT WWW.AMERICANCHILLERS.COM TO ORDER YOURS!

join the official

AMERICAN CHILLERS

FAN CLUB!

**Visit
www.americanchillers.com
for details!**

About the cover art: This unique cover was designed and created by Michigan artists Darrin Brege and Mark Thompson.

Darrin Brege works as an animator by day, and is now applying his talents on the internet, creating various web sites and flash animations. He attended animation school in southern California in the early nineties, and over the years has created original characters and animations for Warner Bros (Space Jam), for Hasbro (Tonka Joe Multimedia line), Universal Pictures (Bullwinkle and Fractured Fairy Tales CD Roms), and Disney. Besides art, he and his wife Karen are improv performers featured weekly at Mark Ridley's Comedy Castle over the last six years. Improvisational comedy has provided the groundwork for a successful voice over career as well. Darrin has dozens of characters and impersonations in his portfolio and, most recently, provided Columbia Tri-Star pictures with a Nathan Lane 'sound alike' for Stuart Little. Speaking of little, Darrin and Karen also have a little son named Mick.

Mark Thompson has been in the illustration field for over 20 years, working for everyone from the Detroit Tigers, Ameritech, as well as auto companies and toy companies such as Hasbro and Mattel. Mark's main interests are in science fiction and fantasy art. He works from his studio in a log home in the woods of Hamburg Michigan. Mark is married with 2 children, and says he is also a big-time horror fan and comic collector!

All AudioCraft books are proudly printed, bound, and manufactured in the United States of America, utilizing American resources, labor, and materials.

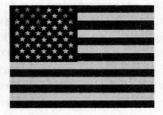

USA